The Pale Girl Murders

Claus Sowalic

AF110423

THE PALE GIRL MURDERS

By Claus Sowalic

All content is purely fictional.

This book has been previously published as "The Girl That Was Obsessed With Murder"

All rights reserved.
Copyright © by Claus Sowalic

No part of this book may be reproduced in any form or by any electronic or mechanical means, including information storage and retrieval systems, without written permission from the author, except for the use of brief quotations in a book review.

ISBN 978-8-3301-2341-5

Table of Contents

Chapter 1: Welcome To Murder 7
Chapter 2: How'd You Know That? 11
Chapter 3: It's In The Attic 17
Chapter 4: Mystery Voice 21
Chapter 5: Get Out Of The Road! 29
Chapter 6: Knocking On Strangers' Doors 33
Chapter 7: Killer Party 37
Chapter 8: Murder Round Two 47
Chapter 9: A Photographer And A Killer 53
Chapter 10: Lunch Plans Down The Drain 57
Chapter 11: Dull Memory, Sharp Evidence 63
Chapter 12: Busted 75
Chapter 13: Framed 79
Chapter 14: No Dead Body Here, That's For Sure 83
Chapter 15: The Interrogation Room 89
Chapter 16: Kate Is Road Kill 97
Chapter 17: The Body Count Rises 103
Chapter 18: Literally A Skeleton In The Closet 107
Chapter 19: Killer Discovery 113
Chapter 20: Waiting Outside Your Window 119
Chapter 21: Tension 123
Chapter 22: Putting The Pieces Together? 135

Chapter 23: You're Seeing A Killer! 141

Chapter 24: Charlie VS. The Darkness 161

Chapter 1: Welcome To Murder

Inside of us lives a battle between good and evil. Where good is, evil tries to follow. Whether or not you believe it, one side will take control. And the worst part is there is only thing that can stop it.

Mary. An innocent girl most of the time. Well, when she wanted. She tried, really did. But she always stirred up trouble. Her distinctive, pale face and baby blue eyes made her easy to spot, and she wore her long blond hair combed to the side to symbolize separating all the bad things in her life from her, like her parents. Neglected. Her brother, who relied on alcohol instead of his parents, spent most of his time behind a jail cell talking to his shadow. She was an interesting girl, Mary. A real character. Things changed when Sophie came into her life. "Imaginary friend?" Please. There was nothing imaginary about Sophie—or friendly. It was when she realized how dysfunctional her family really was when Mary started letting the wrong things—and people— in. One night Mary died. She's still here, though. She knows what's about to happen, and who is behind it all. It's the beginning of a twisted game, and Mary can't do anything to help. All she can do is watch and pray nobody gets hurt too bad.

The air was muggy that night. The streets so silent you could hear the flickering of the old street lamps, which, like the neighborhood, was rotting. As the sun left, dark clouds emerged. If only that was all that happened that night.

Mary stood outside talking with Sophie—soggy leaves breaking under her shoes—and she pouted when she felt a raindrop land on the tip of her cool nose. She had no desire to go inside to the small, yellow house and listen to her parents fighting. It was already enough they didn't realize their daughter was out here alone without any supervision. But she wasn't alone; she had Sophie. She figured one more toss of the red bouncy ball wouldn't hurt. Sophie ran three steps, reached her arm back, and released the ball towards Mary. But Mary knew something was wrong. The ball didn't stop.

"Sophie help!"

It was like Sophie wanted the ball to roll onto the road ahead. She stayed still. Mary felt something inside of her push forward, like she lost control of herself, and soon she was sprinting to the ball, which had halted in the middle of the road.

"Watch out," Sophie whispered before disappearing.

The girl's eyes bulged and she froze as her hand touched the muddy, slimy rubber ball. At first she questioned if she was seeing Heaven. It must have been God telling her He existed, since she had been questioning it lately, even at her young age. A second later, two tires appeared under the Heaven-like headlights, with no intention of slowing down. It must have been the now pouring rain that made the car slip and slide against the sides of the road.

"I got it, Sophie," Mary said to herself before attempting a grip on the ball.

Her black Sketchers slipped from under her, scraping her knee and giving her seconds to dodge the speeding vehicle. It was too late. Mary's body was taken with the car, crushing and cracking it on impact. Her forehead smashed the windshield and thousands of glass particles made their way into her eyes. The car reached a stop at once and Mary's body, now almost in two, rolled off onto the ground and into the mud. Mary was dead.

The driver opened the door too shaken to realize an empty beer can now broken on the ground. They slurred several cuss words, ones Mary often heard her parents yell. The driver picked up what was left of Mary, now smeared with dark blood from the impact, and walked near the parkway bridge under a stream. Mary's body was placed in the red-streaked water, and sunk at once. The sobbing and chaotic driver rubbed his bloody hands together and looked at the stream with curiosity. Not noticed by the driver, a strand of Mary's blond hair surfaced—but it looked black. Maybe it wasn't Mary anymore.

Chapter 2: How'd You Know That?

Charlie Stillman ran his 11-year-old legs down the squeaky wooden stairs of his small, brick home.

"Bye mom," he said before reaching for the door.

His mom, Clare, who was dressed in a pink robe and slippers, chased behind him with a paper bag in her hand.

"Charlie, your lunch!" she said before peering at an empty street, no kids or school bus in sight. She sighed and before the shut the door, something caught her eye. A girl, nine years old perhaps, was glaring back at her with black eyes and through her blonde hair that was combed forward, hiding her forehead. She had unhealthily pale skin, and had legs resembling pool cues. Clare questioned if the girl had been there a moment before. She didn't look intent on catching the bus, considering she just stood at the opposite side of the road, staring. Clare's stomach kicked, and she forced the door close. Distracted by the girl, Clare grunted and looked down at the toy soldier dug into her heel. Behind her walked a teenage girl talking on the phone in a pair of short jean shorts and a pink tank top twirling her brown hair in her finger. Clare picked up a small blue baby blanket and threw it over the sleeping child in the living room. Clare could not help but smile at the precious child's face, but; her smile disintegrated at the picture of a man above the crib. The man appeared to be in his forties and had blinding teeth. Clare forced herself to stop staring and continued on.

Charlie eyed the clock. It was 3:28 PM. He was listening to one of his classmates' presentations on president Lincoln when all he could think about was how his mother had not packed him a lunch, and what he would give for a Happy Meal. The bell rung on cue and the kids flooded out of the building. When Charlie approached his street, a pair of high heels stomped behind him. It was odd considering there was never any sign of life on his street when Charlie walked home. He looked back, seeing everything but a pair of high heels. He shrugged then walked down the rest of the street, approaching his home. He still couldn't shake the feeling of someone following him. He took out a house key from his backpack and heard it *click* in the door. He shut the door, and right behind him in the driveway, staring, stood Sophie.

Clare met Charlie's eyes and held a paper bag to her chest.

"Forget something?"

"Sorry," he said.

"You must be starving. You can finish this after you change the light bulb in the attic."

Clare handed him a 70-watt light bulb and he took several steps before pulling a string hanging from the ceiling, revealing a staircase. The attic was small, as expected, and had light shining from downstairs anyway, making Charlie question why there needed to be a light bulb in the first place. He hunched forward to prevent hitting his head against the inward-sloped ceiling, and shoved two dusty boxes—one containing baseball gloves, basketballs, and numerous yard tools— out of his path to the light bulb. Without worry, Charlie began to replace the light bulbs before feeling a tingle in his palm. The new bulb attracted an orange, florid color and there was a high pitch whistle. The bulb hissed and seared Charlie's hand, making him drop the old light and send glass shattering. The now-red bulb continued to shake. Charlie jumped the staircase and left the attic-way open, hearing an explosion behind him. While he ran for cold water, a strand of blonde hair hung from the attic opening.

After about twenty minutes of ice water, Clare reached for her purse: "Keep the ice on it. You'll be fine. I'm going on a grocery run. Lock the door behind me."

Clare closed the door and drove down the empty street. Charlie walked to the door when he saw a young girl dressed in white from head to toe. Something in Charlie pushed him forward, and his hands fell to his waist, dropping the bag of ice.

"Hi there," the girl said in a polite tone.

"Hey," Charlie said.

"What's your name?"

Something told Charlie he wasn't supposed to talk to strangers, but this girl looked so pure and nice he couldn't help it.

"Charlie, what's yours?" he asked.

"Mary. Sometimes I go by Sophie," the girl spoke while forming a smile that Charlie couldn't tell if he was scared of or fascinated by.

"Why do they call you that?"

The girl paused and ignored Charlie's question, his arm capturing her attention.

"What happened?" she looked sincere and concerned.

"Oh, that. I just...it was a freak thing. It feels a little better now. So, do you live around here?" Charlie pointed around the neighborhood even though he doubted she did. Hardly anyone left his or her houses.

"I do now," Mary said without looking at Charlie.

She stood fascinated with the home.

"Who lives in there with you?"

"Just my mom, brother, and sister."

"No dad?" she asked.

Charlie swallowed a lump in his throat that he thought was an Adam's apple growing in.

"No," he forced out.

"Are your parents divorced?" she kept asking. Charlie looked up at the sky.

"No, he died."

Mary took a step back, but something about her looked like she wanted to ask more questions about him.

"Oh, I'm sorry. I didn't know."

Mary only looked in Charlie's eyes after she said something, but she sounded so convincing, like she actually cared.

"How could you have," Charlie mumbled.

Mary shot him a smile and touched his arm. Charlie felt her touch and dropped the ice bag, but she kept holding on. Her hand tightened brushed against his fingers. A moment after, Charlie bent down to the bag and Mary's grip became lose.

"Do you know how he died?" she asked. Mary could see Charlie struggling, but something was making her ask more questions. His eyes began to water, and she found it hard to look at him after the questions she continued to ask.

"Nope. One day he's here, and the next he isn't. He just disappeared."

Charlie took a step back and began to turn his back against Mary.

"Then how do you know he's not still alive?" she asked.

Charlie bit his lip and didn't even turn around.

"I don't think so. I gave up on that a long time ago. Sorry, I just don't like talking about it. Besides, we would probably would have heard about it from some of our relatives."

Mary looked strangely curious and stared at him with wider eyes: "Like your Aunt Ella?"

She took a second to wonder if she had said that, almost like she was scared.

"How do you know that?" Charlie turned back around, staring at the girl.

She must have realized how she was acting, so Mary shot a sincere, apologetic look at Charlie.

"I'm really glad I met you, Charlie. You're different. I'll see you around?" she asked, holding her hands together in anticipation of his answer.

"Yeah, I guess," he said, and turned around, closing the door for the final time.

There was no sign of Mary outside.

Chapter 3: It's In The Attic

Charlie, still confused, took his hand off the doorknob and saw Kate on the phone.

"Okay I'm on my way," she said.

"Who was that?" Charlie asked.

"Mom. I'm going to pick her up from the hospital," she said while panicking to find her keys.

"What's wrong? What happened to her?"

Charlie put out his hands and his eyes bulged out. His hands began to sweat thinking of what might have happened to his mother.

"She didn't say she just wanted me to hurry."

Kate ran out of the door, forgetting to close it. Charlie stuffed a baby blue pacifier into crying Nick's mouth. Charlie stared at the innocent child, and wondered what it would be like to have another baby around the house. He couldn't help but worry for his mother. He would somehow blame himself if something happened to the baby. Charlie's thoughts shifted from his mother to the girl he had earlier met outside his house. The way she seemed to approach Charlie from nowhere, and know all about him was so weird. It didn't make sense. He had never met the girl before, and she knew things about his family only they knew. He walked past Nick's crib and towards a black Dell sitting on a small desk in the corner of the room. Several names came to mind when thinking of the girl, but Charlie later remembered and typed *Mary—Denver, Colorado*," and anticipated what might come up.

He clicked on several links but nothing connected with the same girl he had talked to. Of course the Internet would hopefully not have pages dedicated to a nine-year-old girl living in Colorado but it was worth a try. He shut the computer, hearing it shut. For a moment, he heard the same noise of the computer shutting. He waited a second, but something made another noise. He looked over Nick in his crib incase it was him, but he was already back asleep. It must have been Kate back from the hospital already.

"Kate? Are you already back with mom?"

There was no reply. Charlie turned off the heat to make sure he wasn't just hearing that, but the source of the noise, at this point it was almost like a hum, seemed to be the attic. Sophie's thin, cold voice echoed within Charlie's ear: *Like your Aunt Ella?* The question repeated in his head, each time in a higher pitch and with an added giggle at the end. The laugh turned into a scream, and soon Charlie's thinking was clogged by a girl's scream that sounded like she scared and running for survival. Charlie questioned if it was just in his head or if there, somewhere in the house, was in fact someone screaming. Charlie touched his ears but the screams got louder. They were coming from the attic. Charlie took the first step up the wooden, splinter-infested way to the attic. The screams made him lose his balance, and he was forced to grab onto the upper step. He raised his head but a scream shattered his brain and Charlie fell off the ladder onto the hardwood floor. The television boomed and Charlie found himself on his feet seeing a frantic girl screaming on the screen. The only other person in the house was Nick, who remained in his crib. He unplugged the television and a moment later the voices were silenced.

The front door creaked. Clare stood disheveled with messy hair and red eyes that must have spent time crying.

"Mom what happened?"

She took her feet out of her worn out shoes and turned to Charlie.

"I was worried. My stomach was killing me and I didn't want to take chances," she said.

"What did they say?" Charlie asked.

He took her coat and motioned for her to sit down.

"It's only serious if the pain continues. The doctor said it might harm the baby eventually. I don't want to talk it about it anymore. Where's CJ?" she squeaked.

"He just woke up. I think he's hungry."

Clare dropped her purse in the middle of the kitchen floor and tended to the crib.

Chapter 4: Mystery Voice

As Clare tried to sleep, lightning bolts continued flashing her eyes open—open to the past. Clare's mind focused on the police officer at her door that night: *We've tried everything but we will not give up. I'm so sorry.* She impulsively threw the covers off of her sweaty body and ran to the bathroom with her hand covering her bloated stomach. Behind her, for a mere second, an outline of a figure stood for the second-long lightning flash.

Clare knelt, holding up the toilet seat as she vomited for what seemed like the whole night.

When the sun rose, Charlie shielded his red and exhausted eyes from the blinding light. With one eye open, he moved down the stairs to see a sobbing Kate hiding a tissue crumbled in her hand.

"She didn't want to wake you. You seemed tired," she said.

Charlie shot her a confused look while running his hand through his morning-Mohawk.

"Mom might have lost him last night."

The words acted as an alarm clock for Charlie and he moved his hand from his hair to over his mouth.

"She doesn't know for sure though."

Kate looked at the ceiling and sniffled. She held back tears and Charlie could tell she wanted to change the subject, as did he.

"There's that girl again. What was her name again?" Kate asked.

She was referring to the small, nine or ten-year-old girl who stood outside the window and across the street. She wore a black dress that looked like it had been through hell. She began to turn her face towards Kate when she motioned for Charlie to look. Charlie pushed the curtains to the side to see a rotting house with dead plants surrounding it across the empty street.

"What girl?" Charlie shot her a blank stare waiting for a reply.

Kate pointed across the street: "She was just here a second ago."

"Did she have blonde hair?"

"Yeah, why?"

"Her name is Mary, I think," he said staring at the wall.

"Well she doesn't have much of a wardrobe considering she's wearing the same black dress she wore yesterday. She doesn't look like a Mary."

Kate closed the curtains. The smell of burnt movie popcorn permeated the room.

"Did you leave a stove on?" Kate asked.

Charlie shook his head and began walking around the kitchen corner.

"It's coming from the attic!"

Kate grabbed a handful of towels and began climbing the ladder to the attic, seeing a box in flames at the center of the small room. From the last step of the ladder, Kate threw the towels on top of the box.

"Charlie get some water!"

She threw her frantic body back down the stairs and reached for a bucket. She stopped coughing from the smoke for a moment. Charlie followed behind Kate climbing up the ladder until something wet hit his arm: it was Kate's bucket.

"What was that for?"

Charlie looked up to his sister who was just standing there as a box was on fire.

"You aren't going to believe this"

Charlie finished the last step and stood in awe also: the fire was gone. Not only that, but there no sign of a fire. The smoke was gone, the air was clear, and the box itself looked untouched. There was one sign of the fire— a burnt picture of a man sitting on the top of the box.

"What just happened?" Kate asked.

"Did we do something wrong? What's been going on with this house? Maybe this place is haunted or something."

Charlie saw the crazy look Kate gave him.

"Think about all the crazy things that have happened in the past few days. How else do you explain all of this?"

Kate became frustrated not being able to explain it.

"I don't know, alright. Don't you realize that mom will kill us when she finds out that picture is ruined?"

The two shot each other questions for the majority of the night—without any being answered. As Kate walked outside the bathroom door after brushing her teeth, she heard something that sounded like footsteps. The noise was too heavy to be Charlie's feet. She reached for her lamp, turning the power switch. The lamp sparked and she was sent into darkness. Her left pinky skimmed the door handle, and she pulled the door behind her. Without a weapon in hand, she continued walking down the hallway. The noise increased—something was at the front door. Kate turned her feet around the corner with panic on her face, but through the door walked a disheveled Clare, whose makeup was smeared, eyes were bloodshot, and hair was greasy and wet. Kate had seen her mother bad off before, and she was concerned, but it was when she looked down from her face that her heart stopped for a moment.

Clare's figure looked like it had six months ago—before she found out she was pregnant. Kate covered her mouth, which was wide open. For the next couple days, Kate tried to explain what had happened to Charlie, but all he was concerned about was that his mother was still in her bedroom, sobbing. The two, feeding CJ, sat by the kitchen table.

"What was that?" Kate asked, hearing some sort of alarm.

The answering machine sounded: *Hey Clare, it's Victor. I just missed your call, it sounded important. You didn't sound too good; call me when you get this. Bye.*

"Who's Victor?" Kate asked.

"Maybe someone she works with. We probably should have not listened to it."

Kate rolled her eyes and Charlie left his fork on his full plate and headed to the garage. He rolled out with a helmet on his head and pedals under his feet. The air was foggy, and the ground was muddy. Charlie put his bike on the road and began peddling faster with every rotation. His vision blurred as he tried to maneuver the bike in the endless fog. He turned at what seemed like a left corner when something forced him to crush the brake level and fly forward. It was Sophie.

"Sorry, did I scare you? I can't see anything in all this fog."

"No, I was going too fast," Charlie said before shifting his bike in the opposite direction and sitting back down.

"Are you okay? You seem possessed to get home or something."

"C'mon, how would I be possessed?"

"I'm just asking. You never know, it could happen. You still look scared, but of what?"

"Well, I'm scared of spiders, does that count?"

"I hate spiders. Is your mom okay?"

Charlie looked back confused but couldn't see anything except fog.

"When did you see my mom?"

"She was crying when I saw her walking to your house today."

"Why were you watching our house?"

Charlie directed the bike towards her again and his stare became more serious. The girl seemed to have endless questions but no answers. She placed her small white hand on top of his bony right shoulder, showing her newly painting black nails.

"You seem really jumpy. Are you sure you're okay?"

Charlie shoved her hand off of his shoulder and capped his head with his dark blue helmet.

"Look, I need to get back home. I'll see you later, I guess."

He began peddling, hopefully, towards his house. After a few moments he looked back but Sophie was gone. The fog must have just been too thick.

Once home, Charlie reached for Kate, who gave him a strange look.

"Where were you for so long?" she asked.

"It took me awhile. The fog is crazy."

Kate glanced out the window. Her nose wrinkled as she saw hardly any fog outside, and merely some clouds. She looked at Charlie, but didn't feel like diving into that.

"Did you talk to mom about all the weird stuff that's been happening?"

"Yeah. She wasn't as mad about the picture as I thought she'd be. She's still to upset over the baby. But she said she would hear us out and think about it."

"That's a good start. I want to go home, though."

"Even though..." Kate stopped.

"Yes. Don't you think forgetting about dad maybe wasn't the brightest idea we had? This could be a sign we shouldn't separate ourselves from those memories. It's not like this house is helping anything."

"You're right. Lets sleep on it and talk more in the morning."

"All right, goodnight," Charlie said before covering himself with his bright red covers.

Chapter 5: Get Out Of The Road!

By four in the morning, Charlie had still not slept at all. He tossed and turned in his bed, kicking off almost all the covers. Flashes of Sophie didn't just pop up in his mind but were *burnt* in it. He couldn't shake the image of her. There was something so strange about her—Charlie had never met a girl like her. The way she seemed to have nothing to do but watch his house and somehow knew more about Charlie's life than he did practically. He just didn't get it. How could this stranger know so much about him? These thoughts sent chills up Charlie cold back. A police car alarmed in the street and Charlie jumped. The red and blue lights made him raise his right arm over his eye. He crawled out of bed and shoved his curtains to the side.

There was no cop car in sight but a soaking-wet Sophie outside of his window. She stood there, staring. It looked like a statue. The liquid pouring onto her turned red. She closed her eyes and held her hand up to him, staring. Charlie covered the window back and shot to his bed, not caring if she was still there. He forced his eyes to close and he rolled up in his thick comforter. He stayed like that for the rest of the night.

When the sun finally came up, Clare began packing. She started with her red, solid jacket then moved to her stacks of pink-dotted, no-show socks. Within minutes she had torn the room apart with all the clothes, many of which were stained with mascara that had ran from Clare's eyes. She never thought a person could physically cry that much. Kate and Charlie soon walked in.

"What's going on?" Kate asked.

"Where are we going?" added Charlie.

"Home."

The kids exchanged looks then stared at Clare's suitcase, which was just about full.

"As in the home we lived in with...dad?"

The kids didn't fully understand. Clare must have come to her senses and realized the house was haunted. They weren't complaining. They just figured it would have taken more than a day to convince her. Clare gave Kate a nod.

"How come?"

"This house just isn't working for us. And with what's happened, I need the support of not only you guys but Veronica and everyone back home more than ever."

Veronica was Clare's best friend. They had both been there for the other for pretty much everything.

"Go get packed," she whispered before returning to her suitcase.

"Well that was easy," Charlie said.

"Ow! What the hell?" Kate said.

She looked down at her foot, which stepped on a broken beer bottle. Blood began to ooze out and she motioned for Charlie to fetch some paper towels.

"I know she can drink now, but don't you think it's a little soon to..."

Clare walked in. Kate hid her foot around the corner and wiped the pain expression off of her face.

"Kate, I completely forgot about my car. Would you go pick it up from the hospital?"

She hardly looked at Kate. Instead she talked to the ground, like she was too ashamed of losing a baby to look at her own daughter.

"Be right back."

The bus Kate rode to the hospital came to a red light. The bus smelled stale and like old people and sweat. Her body shifted forward as the bus stopped, and she looked at her foot. Even through she had wrapped it she could still see blood from the wound. She didn't think a broken bottle could do that kind of damage. She couldn't believe what she saw when she looked up from her foot: Sophie. She must have bought new clothes because she stood in the middle of the intersection in a long white gown peering through all the people in the bus, straight at Kate. Kate saw the light next to her turn green and she rose from her seat. Sophie continued staring at Kate like a statue; but the longer Kate starred the more she could distinguish a scared look on her face. The little girl almost looked helpless, but Kate didn't know what to do. Before she could think any more the black SUV sped up and approached the center of the intersection. Kate felt like screaming something to the bus driver but it wouldn't do anything. A moment later the car sped into Sophie's body. Had the driver not seen the girl? If Kate could see it at the back of a tinted bus so could he. Kate closed one eye and moved out in the aisle of the bus. She couldn't believe it: Sophie was fine. The small girl didn't even move; but the car had run into her. Kate held onto the pole against her seat. She looked again at the girl, now holding a red bouncy ball. Kate could have sworn she hadn't been holding that a second ago. She looked up and saw her stoplight turn green, and felt the bus shifting. Kate was frantic and looked at everyone else on the bus, who were either reading, playing on their phone, or listening to music. When she lacked up at Sophie she was gone. It was like she was never there. Kate sighed and buried herself within her jacket while putting her hands on her head.

Chapter 6: Knocking On Strangers' Doors

"Mom?" Charlie said as he knocked on Clare's door. She could tell she was on the phone with someone, but he didn't want to ease drop. He did hear, though, something like *Of course I didn't. That was never part of the plan.* As he was about to leave her door he heard it unlock and Clare's head pop out.

"What?"

"Well, I'm all packed," Charlie said innocently.

Clare flashed him a smile.

All Kate could think about was that little girl while she pulled out of the hospital parking lot. Had she gone mad? She didn't even feel like she was driving but as if she was in some kind of trance. She must have hit a speed bump or something because she felt her car stop but when she finally looked again she saw her car smashed against the back of the vehicle parked in front of her. She turned down the radio and went into panic mode. Seeing Sophie messed with her head. As an impulse, Kate revved the car in reverse and pulled out of the parking lot, without noticing the security camera above her.

Clare heard the garage door. Charlie caught her: "Mom, why exactly are we going back home?"

"We will talk about that later Charlie right now I'm busy," she said before opening the door to the garage.

Kate took out the key of the car and read the look on her mother's face.

"Before you freak, it's really not that bad and I didn't get hurt."

"How did this happen?" "I was distracted for like less than one second, I swear. I had to dodge this tree that fell right in the road. I'll pray for the damage."

"At least you are okay. It isn't that bad, anyway. We can definitely still drive it home. We'll worry about it then. For now, let's get everything in the car!"

After hours of Clare making sure they had every little thing, they were ready to leave. As they drove out of the neighborhood, Charlie saw Mary in a white dress staring at him with a rather pouty look on her face. She looked like she was about to wave, but he couldn't tell because he turned his cheek and looked straight ahead.

"Aren't you going to answer that mom?"
Kate always made fun of mom's default-ring-tone.

"Today is about us," she said, flashing him a smile in the mirror.

After what seemed like forever they arrived home...actual home.

"Here we are!" Clare yelled.

The Victorian-styled house was pink and outdated but spacey and had a huge, winding driveway approaching several wooden steps. There was a huge backyard behind the house, too. The inside was still mostly furnished. Charlie lifted a box with the majority of his room inside of it and saw a shovel in his mother's hands.

"I was thinking about picking up gardening again. Your dad and I used to have that garden overflowing with all kinds of stuff," Clare said while looking at the ground.

Charlie could tell she missed dad. They all did. Clare checked her phone.

"You okay, mom?" Kate asked.

Clare's face looked concerned staring at the phone.

"Of course," she said, faking a smile and hiding the phone back in her left back pocket in her jeans.

"I'm just glad we are done with that weird girl with the hideous dress," Kate whispered to Charlie.

He nodded. They were both glad they were out of her path. They could focus on themselves now. Although she did look sad when they left, Charlie thought. Maybe she just didn't have any friends and wasn't good at talking to other people. That still wouldn't explain all the stuff she knew about Charlie. It didn't matter, though. It was in the past. Clare pulled the car around the driveway and made her way through the neighborhood. She told the kids she would get groceries considering there was nothing in the refrigerator. She pulled in front of a run-down, moldy brick house. She exited the car and walked up the brick stairs, knocking on the door.

"Oh my gosh, Clare. Hi," a man said.

He was tall, had brown eyes and a rough beard, and looked about 35. He looked down at her stomach.

"We need to talk," she said.

"Yeah, I know. I thought the worst when you weren't answering me."

"I couldn't. Not in front of the kids," Clare said.

"Here, come in," the man said, motioning his hand.

Clare obeyed and shut the door.

CHAPTER 7: KILLER PARTY

"It feels weird to be back here," Charlie said.

"Yeah, well we have the summer to get used to it," Kate said while scraping the place out for some crackers.

"Did you hear that?"

It was the house at the end of the cul-de-sac.

"Looks like some kids messing with Mr. Jones."

Three boys, who were definitely in middle school, ran to the doorbell and pressed it several times, before jumping into the bushes. Charlie's mind went to school. Him and his friends had always laughed at this poor kid who had red hair, glasses, and always were plaid shirts. He did everything the cliché nerd did.

"Charlie?" Kate said.

"Sorry. Mr. Jones doesn't need that."

He closed the curtains.

Clare pulled her grocery cart around the corner into the bread aisle. She reached for a pack and saw a human eye—presumably belonging to a little girl—behind it staring at her. Her hand let go of the bread and she covered her hand over her heart.

"Abigail come on!" a man said from the other side of the aisle.

The girl looked up at her dad.

"Coming dad," she said before wondering off.

Clare sighed and bent down to the bread. She turned another corner, this time bumping with another cart.

"Excuse me," she said looking down as her heart still pounded.

"Clare? Oh my gosh, Clare? Is that you?" a voice said.

She looked up from the ground to see a woman with long, wavy brown hair and thick lips under bright red lipstick. She wore an elegant black and gold-covered dress and gave Clare a smile from ear to ear.

"Vivian!" Clare said.

For the next few minutes the women caught up. They talked about their kids, their busy schedules, and of course, why Clare was there. She looked into Vivian's cart, which held wine bottles and cheese. The woman didn't look like she cared about a thing.

"So listen," she said, "I'm throwing a little summer kick-off party at the house on Friday. All of us miss you, Clare. Would you please come?"

"I don't see a reason to say no," Clare said.

"Great!" "Thanks so much, Vivian. It's great to see you again."

"Oh likewise, dear. I'll see you this Friday," she said with a wink.

Later that evening Clare walked through the front door with bags filled with food in hand.

"Do we have to go?" Kate said when she told them about the party.

"Is it that big of a deal? It will be fun."

Clare handed them the bags and walked to her room.

On Friday, Kate reached for a towel and yelled out to Charlie: "I'm taking a shower, will you take care of CJ?"

Charlie nodded and she closed the door. About an hour later they walked out of their driveway.

"Why didn't we just drive?" Kate said.

"Across the neighborhood?" Clare snapped back.

It was humid, hot, and it felt like there was nothing but stickiness in the air. Kate adjusted her shirt and aired out her arms when she noticed herself starting to sweat.

When everyone else was excited to see Vivian's house, Charlie saw something else. He looked to his left and saw an elderly woman—well most of an elderly woman at least. He couldn't really make out her face. A group of trees were blocking his view. He did see, though, a Bible in the woman's lap as she sat on a wooden porch swing. She wore a plain, white dress that nearly covered her ankles.

"Here we are," Clare said, turning Charlie's shoulder to fix his view on the house.

He looked back at the old woman, but she was gone. At least, he couldn't see her. There were trees blocking his view completely now.

"I want everyone to be on his or her best behavior."

"We know," Kate said.

Charlie turned to the house, still thinking of the woman.

Clare rung the doorbell and Vivian answered with a wine bottle in her hand. She insisted they come in. She wore a long, slimming red dress with sparkles on the right shoulder. Her hair was combed up into a bun-like style. The guests inside spotted the family within seconds. Several adults holding margaritas rushed to Clare, and even Kate saw some of her old friends near the Wii in the family room. Clare gave CJ to Kate and Charlie followed her. Before she could reunite with her friends, a strange woman who looked about sixty who looked like she had been through war approached the kids. She wore a short—too short for an old lady—black dress.

"Hey guys! Kate and Charlie...right? Some people told me you guys were back in town. It's okay if you kids don't remember me, I wouldn't blame you. So you guys are permanently back?"

Kate and Charlie looked at each other.

"It looks like it," Charlie said.

"I'm glad. I don't know what kind of stuff you guys might have dealt with that made you come back, but just don't expect everything to be all peachy now, you know? Every town has its issues, but I'm sure you've figured that out. Anyway, I hope you guys have fun tonight!"

The two kids gave awkward half-smiles and the woman walked away.

"Who was that?"

"Like I knew?" Kate said.

Charlie reached for a cup next to the punch bowl, but Kate touched his arm and stared at the wall in thought.

"There's something weird with her. This town isn't all that big, Charlie. Don't you think we would have at least seen her before? I know we don't remember everyone by heart, but she would have been someone that stuck in my memory. Besides, we at least recognize everyone else at this party."

"You're right," Charlie added.

"Look at her. She sticks out like a sore thumb. That dress is way too short, too. She probably hasn't talked to anyone else here—why choose to talk to us? I'm positive we've never seen her before," Kate said.

Charlie let out a sigh.

"Kate what the hell?" she heard.

Behind her were three familiar faces.

"Kate what are you doing here?" one voice said.

"Are you moving back?" another said.

It was Kate's three best friends. They grabbed her by the hand and told her about how they almost died without her. She handed CJ to Charlie and shot him an apologetic look, knowing he didn't have anyone to talk to. He glanced again by the punch bowl and saw the mysterious old woman glancing at Kate. He turned his eyes back to CJ, seeing the innocence in his eyes and the cute wrinkle in his nose. He also saw a man across from the punch bowl staring at him. Charlie stared back and it took the man a moment before he turned away. The man had a beard, looked like he was in his thirties, and was noticeably under-dressed. Behind him stood a red-haired boy sitting in a wheelchair socializing with two other boys, both holding red cups of punch. Flashbacks ran through Charlie's mind as he noticed the kids, and he felt his stomach swell.

He, still with CJ, ran down the hall to what looked like a bathroom. As he was about to close the door, the weird old woman spoke again.

"Someone often pees heavy in evening."

Excuse me? Charlie thought. What was that supposed to mean?

"Uh, yeah," he mumbled before shutting the door.

"Clare sweetheart can I get you some punch?" Vivian said.

Clare nodded and smiled. She handed her the cup, and their hands brushed against each other.

Charlie turned the light off and opened the bathroom door. The hallway was no longer crowded—he looked around the corner to see all the guests gathered in a circle, staring at something, or someone, on the floor. As he walked forward someone came behind him and covered his mouth, pushing him towards the back door. He looked up from the ground to see Kate, still covering his mouth, motioning for him to stay quiet. She kept her hand over his mouth until they reached their driveway.

"Okay, you can *whisper,*" she said.

She looked at Charlie's horrific and confused face.

"I didn't mean to scare you," she said.

"You did a good job of it. You mind telling me what just happened?"

"I didn't want us to get blamed or sit there being questioned for hours," she said while looking out the curtains and taking CJ from Charlie.

"Blamed for what Kate? What happened?"

She looked him straight in the eyes: "Vivian collapsed."

"What?"

That must have been who everyone was staring at.

"I didn't see it, but people said she was just getting some punch then fell. When I got you they were all scrambling to find a pulse."

"Well wouldn't have been smart to stay and help? Why'd you make us leave?"

"I don't know, I panicked. I figured we would be easy suspects if this turned into a murder case. The two kids who suspiciously came into town a few days before she was killed."

Charlie sat down and looked like Kate had lost her mind.

"Kate, that's ridiculous. Nobody said anything about her being murdered. Besides, we look a lot more suspicious now that we left. What about Mom? She's probably freaking out."

"I'm sorry. But Charlie, you don't understand, I couldn't risk being there if cops came. I didn't tell mom the whole truth about the car being dented. This isn't far from Denver; they could have people looking out for me. I hit another car, not a street light."

Charlie bit his lip.

"I didn't want to leave you alone or have you worrying about me missing," she said as she put her hand on his shoulder.

Charlie rolled her eyes without her noticing.

"I wonder what Mr. Jones did. This is the last thing he needs after just being released from that mental hospital."

"Charlie, it wasn't a mental hospital. It was some therapy office. Their family probably went through some trough stuff and he needed help. I didn't even see him at the party, though."

Before Charlie could say anything, something caught their attention. It was not a knock, but something *hit* the front door.

"You think that's mom?"

"I don't know. Don't you think everyone at the party is getting questioned still? She's going to be so worried about us," Charlie pointed out.

Kate opened the front door without hesitation, but nobody was there.

"You heard that too, right?" Kate asked.

"There's nobody out here," she said.

Kate walked down two of the three brick steps and turned her head—nothing.

"That's weird," Charlie said while stepping forward towards her.

He looked around also.

"Let's go back inside."

Kate walked up the first one, and Charlie followed. He head turned as he heard something in the bushes. A man sprung up and Charlie felt his ankle being grabbed before his entire body was tackled to the cold, stiff grass in the front yard. Kate looked back, horrified. She

Chapter 8: Murder Round Two

"You thought that was funny, huh? Is that what it was?" the man said while he held down Charlie.

The man wore a suit with a black tie now filled with grass stains. He had a buzz cut and had yellow, crooked teeth that were home to breath that smelled like rotten eggs and spoiled milk. He had much more strength than Charlie anticipated.

"Mr. Jones?" he asked under his breath.

Charlie saw his small veins peeping through his skin as they began to turn blue. The man's hold was so tight on him no matter how hard he pushed against him he didn't move off of Charlie.

Kate rushed over and put her hand over the man's shoulder and tried to push him off Charlie. The man's head snapped back.

"What are you talking about Mr. Jones? Please, just let him go!"

"You killed my Vivian. That's what I'm talking about!"

His hold became tighter and Charlie's throat tightened.

"Mr. Jones, we don't have any idea what you're talking—"

The man didn't wait for her to finish.

"Don't act innocent Ms. -center-of-attention. Nobody else left when she fell. I'm not stupid. First my daughter, and now my wife? How much more hell will I have to go through?"

The man pulled out a pocketknife and took it to Charlie's neck.

"You're not taking anything else from me, and I'll make sure of it," he said.

Charlie grabbed Nathan's wrist, but his grip became weaker every second and the knife was lowering towards him.

"I didn't kill her!"

"Liar! All they found on Vivian was a black smear or bruise-like mark on the back of her neck, just like the black stuff smeared on your fingers. I don't understand it but I know you did something to her."

Kate panicked and remembered her mother talking about gardening. She took off her heels and sprinted towards the shovel, tripping on the first step. Charlie kicked his feet and hoped Kate was finding help. Charlie felt the blade of the knife skim his neck and heard Mr. Jones scream. The knife fell from his hands onto the wet ground and behind him stood Kate holding the shovel, breathing harder than never before. She dropped the weapon and lifted the man's feet off of Charlie, allowing him to breathe. The grass soon turned a puddle of red under the man's head. Kate's hands shook and Charlie coughed for what felt like forever.

"We have to get rid of this before someone sees," Kate whispered.

Charlie looked at her.

"Where do we put him?" "Start digging," she said, pointing to the shovel with her shaking finger.

They were in shock. They had just killed a man— a human life was no longer here. They took that away from him. Charlie looked at his hands, seeing the black smears Mr. Jones referenced. Where had that been from? Charlie couldn't help but ask himself: would everyone else in the town believe he killed Vivian also? He wondered if it was a coincidence or if someone had framed him. His attention was directed to Kate who brought two rolls of paper towels to clean the blood dripping from the man's head into the grass.

There wasn't much space to hide the body, but they did have a little patch of trees further back from their backyard they decided to dig him in. All they knew is they had to get it out of the front yard. After a while Charlie dropped the shovel from exhaustion.

"My arms are going to fall off," he said to Kate, who was hiding the traces of the bloody paper towels.

"Oh my gosh Charlie, did he get you?" she asked.

His face was confused until she placed one of the paper towels up to his neck and looked at the red spot on it.

He placed his finger on his neck, where Mr. Jones' knife had barely, just barely, skimmed the top.

"What am I going to tell mom?" he asked.

"We will figure it out, for now go make sure I got all of the blood from the grass. I'll finish digging," she said.

Kate made sure the body was not visible from any angle, and washed the blood off of the shovel. The two, exhausted, made their way up the front steps. Charlie dropped the clean roll of paper towels. He turned around and picked them up.

"Oh my gosh, Kate," he said as chills ran up his spine and his pulse quickened.

Kate turned around, too.

"You've got to be kidding me," she said as her feet started to tingle.

"The woman from the party," Charlie whispered, making his hair on his neck rise.

Across the street stood the old lady from the party who somehow knew the two without them ever seeing her before. They couldn't see much more other than her face but she continued staring at them through the curtains.

She had seen everything. She raised her hand half way in the air, almost like a wave.

Chapter 9: A Photographer And A Killer

Kate rushed inside and locked the door.

"Was she there the whole time?" Charlie asked.

"Who cares? We just killed a man!" Kate yelled.

Her arms and voice were shaky.

"Do you think anyone else saw?"

"Charlie we could go to jail, do you realize that?"

"I know, Kate! I'm just thinking, okay? I mean it was in self defense—*he* was trying to kill *me*!"

Charlie walked to the sink and rinsed off the blood.

"But who's going to believe us over an old lady?"

"We need to have our story straight for mom. She's going to be here any second."

"Look how much my arms are shaking!"

"What do I tell mom about my neck?"

Kate thought for a second. She brought back makeup from her room and covered the cut over his throat.

"That's the best we can do," she said.

"Okay but what happens when she tells everyone that we killed Mr. Jones?"

"We'll make sure she doesn't. Leave that to me," Kate said.

Charlie didn't know if Kate fully knew what she was saying. For all they knew half the town could have known about what they just did by now.

"Did you know he had a daughter?" she said, changing the subject.

"Nope. Maybe he made it up," Charlie added.

"It wouldn't surprise me, he just showed me he was crazier than what we thought."

"So what now? We just live with the fact that a body we killed is buried in our yard?"

Kate let out a large sigh and buried her face in her arms. The two changed clothes and ran to their rooms when they heard Clare at the door. They didn't feel like coming up with excuses this late.

Her mascara was smeared and she took three tries to get the key in the hole of the door. The home was dark with the exception of one dim lamp near the kitchen. She called out for Kate and Charlie but there was no answer. She just hoped they were in bed—or at least somewhere in the house. Clare ensured each curtain was closed and each door was locked in the house, and then walked to the kids' rooms. She opened Charlie's first, and saw him in bed rolled over with his back against her. She closed the door and exited—while Charlie sat rolled in his blankets with his eyes wide open, staring outside.

Clare walked into Kate's room—but she was rolled over with her back against her, also wide-awake, but she wouldn't let her mother know that. She heard her mother's footsteps and her hand against her back and immediately shut her eyes. Clare pulled a fallen comforter back over Kate and closed the door behind her. Kate opened her eyes again.

Charlie's body squeaked his bed back and fourth, thinking about what he and Kate had done. They were *murderers.* His mind couldn't wrap around what might happen if his mom—or worse, the police—found the body. There was no way they could hide it—what were they going to do about the smell? Charlie tried to guide his thoughts to anything else, like the fact that it was summer and he didn't have to worry about school. Except he knew he had much more to worry about now. He wanted to check on Kate, but knowing how shaken she probably was, he didn't want to scare her. Throwing the blanket over his head didn't help either—all he could see was Mr. Jones on top of him. His mind was too full to permit thoughts of what happened to Vivian to enter. It sure looked like Charlie's theory that maybe Vivian got back up minutes later and was fine was not proven accurate but instead there really was a murder at the party. Unlike Mr. Jones' assumption, Charlie had no idea what—or who—was the reason for her death, after all he was in the bathroom when she fell. He may have not had a clue—but someone did.

While Charlie spent the night clueless, someone else enjoyed the last sip of fruit punch and placed it on their dark wood desk, which was covered in pictures. There were photos of Vivian, Clare, Charlie, and Mr. Jones, among others. Also on it was a small, red square-shaped earring. They grabbed those of Vivian and threw them in the garbage bin to the side. Seconds later the pictures went into flames as a match went flying into the bin, and the pictures were destroyed.

CHAPTER 10: LUNCH PLANS DOWN THE DRAIN

That morning Clare was quick to turn the TV off. There had been a news reporter speaking about Vivian's death. She said the only evidence on her body was two bruise-like marks and that the only lead police had was Mr. Jones—who was now missing after suspiciously fleeing the scene before the cops came.

"Sorry again about last night Mom," Kate said.

"You have no idea what kind of things ran through my mind. You could have at least called me instead of worrying me sick," Clare said as her head was buried in a pillow on the couch.

Even though it was early, Clare had already had a few shots trying to cope with reality. Kate took advantage of it and made up lies about why they left the night before. Her favorite was that she thought she had left the stove on. Clare was too, well...*everything* to care. She never had this many emotions stirring inside of her—her friend was gone after seeing her one-day. The alcohol had been helping, though. She didn't drink *that* much, but when it was time, it was time.

"As long as it doesn't happen again. We have to be extra careful now."

"You're right. I'll be careful when I'm out with Michelle and them," Kate said as she grabbed her purse and headed towards the door.

Clare called her name.

"You already have plans?" she said.

"It's just lunch. Can I not go or something?" Kate said.

Kate was always sympathetic and nice to her mother, but had to get her way. Sometimes she looked at Clare not as a mother but as a roadblock for fun.

Her mother nodded but told her she'd call if she hadn't heard from Kate after a while. Clare was trying her best—it wasn't easy with everything going on. She remained on the couch, still thinking about Vivian. It wasn't like they were twins—if anything they were complete opposites—but they did have a special friendship, even if it didn't seem like it.

"Hey, Mom," Charlie said.

"You don't have plans to, do you?" she asked.

"I don't really feel like going out," Charlie said, knowing that he didn't have anyone to meet or anywhere to go.

Charlie tended to his room. He heard something outside his window. Reporters pounded the house of the strange man he had seen at the party. For a second he wondered if the mystery was over and they were arresting him for killing Vivian, but there were no police. Charlie kept staring and grabbed a notepad.

"Thank you," Kate said to the waitress as she handed her the raspberry lemonade.

Along with Kate were Michelle, Ashley, and Sydney—Kate's best friends. Michelle was the leader of the group, even though none of them would admit it. She pushed the others to do things they would never do alone, like make out with boys they just met or steal a pack of gum—petty, silly things, but the girls obeyed.

"My mom told me about Mrs. Jones this morning," Michelle said, unrolling the black napkin and sticking her fork into her salad.

"You were at the party, though. Didn't you already know?"

"I didn't hear. I left the party a little early—when I said I needed to pee."

She winked at the girls.

"I went back to Noel's house. I did get the best pictures at the party though—Mrs. Jones looked beautiful."

Ashley, who wore a blue hoodie and had dirty blonde hair, turned to Kate.

"Speaking of being MIA, where were you after Ms. Jones left?"

Kate's face began to blush. She looked down and crunched her lettuce, digging her fork into the plate.

"I wasn't feeling so good."

"Maybe it was that toxin Ms. Jones drank," she said.

Kate let go of the fork.

"Toxin?"

"Relax, it was a joke. You can't say the punch didn't taste like crap. But seriously, what do you think happened to her?"

The waitress brought the girls' entrees. They quieted as she set down the hot plates in front of them.

Kate shook her head and Michelle interrupted, "Hey Kate, you think I could borrow those hot earrings you had on last night sometime?"

There was so much that happened Kate had no idea what earring she wore.

"You know, the red ones?" she asked.

"Oh yeah, sure," Kate said.

After a few minutes the girls placed their napkins over their almost-empty plates. Sydney spent most of the time on her phone, and only talked when the subject wasn't on Vivian.

"I'm going to the bathroom. Who's coming with?" Michelle asked.

Each girl followed, Kate going last, and adjusted their shirts and make-up in the mirror. Michelle put a toothbrush in Kate's hand.

"Well don't just sit there."

Kate gripped the toothbrush, and placed it back in her hands.

"I'm done with that, Michelle," she said.

"Funny because last time I checked you were the one that got us all to do it in the first place. Look at you, practically torturing those jeans of yours. Come on, Kate."

Kate couldn't help but believe all of Michelle's words. She raised her arm and took the brush from Michelle.

"That's my girl," she said.

Chapter 11: Dull Memory, Sharp Evidence

Even when reporters left the man's house, Charlie continued watching. He stared at the window for, well, nothing in particular—anything that might lead him to a clue. He couldn't think straight knowing he may be framed for not only Vivian's murder but Mr. Jones' as well—the police could be there any minute for all he knew. He closed the curtain and set down his pencil, taking a break. He heard the doorbell. Was he about to get arrested? He jumped back on his bed, opened the curtain again, but couldn't see any car parked—but the view from his window was partially blocked from the outside corner of the house. He took a breath, and went for the doorbell. He opened it, staring at the ground.

"Charlie?" a voice said.

He looked up, recognizing it—it was Kate.

He sighed and motioned for her to come in.

"Hey, sorry," he said, his heart still beating.

"What have you been up to?" Kate asked.

"We need to talk."

As they headed towards Charlie's room, they met Clare.

"Vivian's mother called— she needs some help with...everything. I would take CJ but I don't want to wake him up. Would you watch him for a while?"

Her voice was soft and Kate was surprised she wasn't mad about not calling her at lunch.

Kate nodded with a smile, and heard her mother's high heels stomp to the front door. Little did she know her mother had different plans.

"I've been thinking, and watching outside all day for clues or leads of any kind," Charlie said, sounding as much like a detective as he could.

Kate crossed her arms across her chest and chuckled.

"You think you're going to be able to gather clues looking out of a window in broad daylight?"

Charlie tossed his notepad on his desk, suddenly realizing how foolish that may have sounded. Kate glanced at the notes.

"No offense, but I don't think a few houses being approached by reporters and counting how many times a car left a house is much to go off of, Charlie," Kate added.

"You're right, I just don't know what to do at this point. I can't stop thinking what might happen if that lady tells someone what she saw," Charlie said.

"I wanted to talk to you about that. There's only one way to find out."

Charlie gave her a confused, frightened look as he predicted what she might say.

"We go and find out for ourselves," she said.

Charlie threw several excuses, but Kate grabbed her shoes.

"Come on," she said.

"We can't leave CJ."

"He's asleep. It will only take a few minutes. We'll be fine," she said before tying her neon-blue Nike sneakers and opened the front door, making sure it wouldn't wake CJ.

They approached the house and stepped up several creaky porch-steps. Charlie looked at his watch, making sure he kept track of how long they were gone for. Kate knocked on the heavy door, and waited. Charlie's hands began to sweat thinking about how this would play out—they didn't even have a plan for how they would talk to her.

"Hi Ms.—"

"—Meredith," the woman said, scratching her neck.

The first thing he noticed was the pearl necklace she wore.

"Right. Well I'm sure you remember but I'm Kate, and this is Charlie."

"I remember you guys. What do you want?"

The words coming out of her mouth sounded bitter, but something about the way she said them sounded genuine—almost friendly, in an odd way—and not as fake as she sounded last night. Maybe she did just feel lonely and was trying to make conversation with them— but why just them? They hadn't seen her talking to anyone else.

"Well, we were wondering if we could come in and talk to you for a few minutes," Kate said, picking at her nails.

Charlie stayed quiet, thinking. A faint smile formed on Meredith's face, and she motioned for them to come in. Had she, *forgotten* about last night? Maybe she only saw them coming from the backyard heading inside—and nothing else. Still, she could tell the cops that they left the party early, but then again, *she* left early too. He looked back at his watch. One minute felt like forever; he hoped CJ was still asleep.

"Well, honey of course. But I was just on my way to water those plants I got in the backyard before I forget again—I've got the memory of a squirrel. Only got room in my mind to remember the really important stuff, you know?"

Kate gave her a nervous laugh, probably thinking the same thing as Charlie.

"You can come in if you don't mind waiting a few minutes," she said.

"Sounds great," Kate said with a smile.

The woman walked outside towards the backyard.

Charlie could tell Kate was thinking the same thing: did Meredith forget about what she had seen?

Either way, it felt weird for them to be in the house without the woman there. It was so...quiet. Charlie watched as Kate found her way to the kitchen.

"What are you doing?" he asked.

"I just want a drink," she said, almost snapping at him.

She opened the black refrigerator door and eyed a glass Coke bottle. She reached for it and struggled to open it.

"Maybe you should wait until she comes back in," Charlie said, looking out the nearest window.

"Relax," she said, looking for a bottle-opener. She tried several cabinets—first seeing one filled with plates, the next with silverware. The third; however, was more interesting.

"Charlie, come see this," she said.

Still looking over his shoulder out the window, he followed to see Kate pulling out a knife from one of the cabinets.

"Kate, what are you doing?" he asked.

She motioned for him to move closer to her and she pointed something out on the knife: the initials *VJ.*

Clare sat at a dark brown dining room table across from a familiar face—for her. It was the man Charlie had seen at the party, who had given him a strange look—and the man who was at the top of Charlie's suspect list. Meredith may have seen Charlie and Kate kill a man, but all his theories about Vivian came back to that man—for now. There was just something weird about him for Charlie.

"Victor, you're acting crazy. Reporters have been pounding everyone," Clare said, taking a sip from her glass.

"Not everyone," the man said.

Clare bit her lip.

"How do you think it looks when I'm the only one missing from the time she fell Clare?"

"You weren't." Clare replied.

She told him about Kate and Charlie, and admitted they had not yet been questioned or pounded by the news or anything.

"That's because you've got such good kids. Nobody would ever accuse them," Victor said.

Clare sighed and stared at the table.

"Yeah, they're more good than I am alright. I still need to tell them everything. How am I supposed to after all of this though?

Victor got up and put his hand on Clare's shoulder.

"Look at me. Everything will be fine, okay? They'll catch whoever is out there, and everything will go back to the way it was before."

Clare grabbed his hand and wrapped it around to the other shoulder.

"I wish it was that simple."

Charlie stared at the knife in Kate's hand.

"You're thinking the same thing as me, right?" Kate asked.

Vivian Jones, Charlie thought as he looked at the letters once more. Somehow this seemed too convenient: had they already found out who killed Vivian?

"It's definitely not hers, but why would she have Vivian's knife?" Charlie asked.

"Maybe she took it as a souvenir after she killed her."

"Come on, Kate. There is no evidence that proves a knife killed her—remember what Mr. Jones said?"

Then again, Mr. Jones hadn't seemed like the most trustworthy—or sane—person around.

"First of all, let's not bring him up at all..."

Before she could finish, Charlie interrupted.

"She's coming!" Charlie said after seeing Meredith place down a hose out of the window.

"What should we do with this?"

"We take it," Kate said.

She saw the expression on Charlie's face that looked like she had said something crazier than Mr. Jones might have.

"This could potentially be evidence. Charlie, we could be the ones to solve this."

Charlie rolled his eyes—he wasn't convinced.

"She's going to see it's gone. And don't you think if she somehow killed her with this knife she would hide it better than in the cabinet?"

Since it was a good point and a flaw in Kate's thinking—she ignored the comment and wrapped the weapon in napkins and placed it in her purse. They heard the doorknob twist as they ran back to the living room.

"Sorry for holding you guys up!"

"Not a problem," Charlie said, finally talking to her.

Kate showed the Coke bottle to her.

"Hope you don't mind," she said.

The woman shrugged and smiled.

"Well I guess we should talk about whatever you kids came here to," she said.

She motioned for them to sit down and they sunk into a leather, expensive-looking couch. Kate started the conversation.

"You said you had a bad memory, but you remembered our names and everything at the party."

"Well I said I remember the important things, didn't I?" she said back to her.

"Sorry, we are just having trouble remembering meeting you."

When she said this, Meredith sat back and slouched down into the plush cushion.

"Well with all that you two have been through I'm sure your memory is a little hazy."

Meredith almost looked offended that they had not recognized her. After a small pause, Charlie joined the conversation.

"Do you have any family?"

Meredith chuckled by this. "Hardly. Not like yours, that's for sure. But I'm all alone in this house."

Her eyes caught Kate's purse, which she held close to her, almost like she was protecting it.

"That's a very pretty purse you have there."

She reached out and touched the soft leather, stroking it.

"Oh, thank you," Kate said as she gently pulled it back to her as Meredith nearly grabbed it. Kate reached out her phone.

"I'm so sorry. We were supposed to be home a long time ago. Our mom is really upset. We'll have to finish this up later, if that's okay?"

At once she backed off of the purse and looked up at Kate. "Of course. Well it was good to see you kids again," she said, walking them out.

"You too," Charlie said softly.

The two walked out, shutting the door behind them. Meredith's smile continued for several more seconds, and she walked in the direction of a hallway at the corner of the room.

"What nice, innocent kids. I don't know what you see in them. They don't look like they could hurt a fly, and they can't take the blame for their family. Whatever you've already done, I don't know—but please, just don't hurt them, all right? She said across the still, tranquil house. There was no reply.

CHAPTER 12: BUSTED

"I can't believe you did all of that, Kate. Instead of asking her about seeing us you stole a possible murder weapon! Did you ever think you could be accused if someone sees you with that?"

"Did what Charlie? Solve Vivian's murder? We are going to be heroes. People will love us. As far as seeing us goes, I think she answered that for us——she hardly remembers anything! If we go back *you* can ask her if she saw us."

Kate kept her purse glued against her hip and moved a piece of hair from her eyes.

"I don't feel like a hero, I feel like a thief."

"Would you calm down? I'm the one who took it. We just have to figure out how to prove she killed her, and do it fast before she can get us arrested."

"We can't just give it to the police. Since it probably *didn't* kill *her*, it would hurt us more than it would help," Charlie said.

Kate was going to add something else, but her attention was towards their front door—which they saw was open.

"Did mom beat us home?" Kate asked.

The two walked into the house. Charlie pushed the door back.

"Mom?" Charlie said.

They noticed how quiet CJ was.

"Told you it was okay leaving him here," Kate said.

Charlie didn't say anything. Why had the door been opened?

He looked at the kitchen countertop, seeing the red house key sitting there.

"Kate how could you not lock the door!"

A moment later he heard Kate.

"Charlie...please tell me you have CJ."

Kate's voice was fragile and broken. Charlie walked to Kate and bent over the crib—seeing it empty.

"Oh my gosh. Do you realize what you've done, Kate?"

She searched frantically all over the house, checking her room first. She then ran to Charlie's, the basement, and Clare's room. She saw the hat CJ had worn earlier sitting on her mother's bed.

"We have to go look for him," Kate said, running towards the garage with her car keys in hand.

She opened the door to the garage, seeing Clare frowning at her and holding CJ in her arms. Kate dropped the keys and let out a breath that lasted ten seconds.

"Scary thought, isn't it? That might have been reality, Kate. Where could you have possibly gone?"

"Mom, I'm sorry. I forgot something at the restaurant," Kate said.

"Why couldn't Charlie stay here?" Clare asked, raising her arms up in anger.

Kate was speechless. No lies were coming to her brain at all. She lowered her head.

"I don't...I don't know. I'm sorry," she said while looking at an oil stain at the garage floor.

Clare sighed and told Kate she couldn't take having a missing child's case on top of worrying about Vivian's funeral, too. She never thought she would have to attend a friend's funeral—not for at least thirty years, anyway.

That night, Kate was too focused on her hot pillow and sweaty pillows to sleep. She thought about her father. Could his death be somehow connected with what was going on now? Flashes of Vivian burnt into her mind—then her father. Memories of the two clogged her mind, but she never remembered them talking much. It was mainly Clare who adored Vivian, not really their father.

"So those were the right ones?" Mr. Stillman said to Kate as she opened up a pair of yellow earrings out of a small, blue box.

"I love them. But daddy, where is the matching necklace you promised to get me?" Kate said back, smiling as if she was waiting for him to show it behind his back.

"Honey I completely forgot. I'm so sorry...but I promised, didn't I?"

Her mother's words never left Kate's mind. *Please stay, Robert. We are about to cut the cake.* If only he had listened. Kate knew her father loved her—enough to drive across town in the rain to pick her up a necklace she didn't even need. If only she knew what her father had been drinking in the car.

She thought of the knife from Meredith, and was glad she stole it. If somehow this murder was related to her father, and this person killed him too—she would stop at nothing to make them pay, even if this was just the first step.

CHAPTER 13: FRAMED

Early that morning, Kate's phone rung and vibrated across her nightstand so hard it fell to the floor. It didn't wake her up—considering there was no way she was going to get any sleep for a long time—but it did scare her. The letters were blurry but she could tell it was Michelle calling.

"Hello?" she said while running her hand through her uncombed hair.

She remained quiet for several moments, hearing all that Michelle had to say. Then she nearly dropped her phone, feeling fully awake now.

"Don't worry, I'm not calling about those earrings you still haven't let me try," Michelle said in a hasty voice.

"Is that what you're calling me for?" Kate said in a friendly way, getting out of bed. She reached for her jewelry box, trying to find the earrings. In the usual spot she found one only.

"No, it's not," Michelle said, this time sounding scared.

Kate looked through her box and even on the floor, but she could not find the second earring.

"What?" she said moments later in a voice that probably scared Charlie across the hall.

Clare picked up her mug of coffee and looked at the newspaper, first seeing a picture of Vivian then of Mr. Jones. She turned away once she saw a picture of Mr. Jones with the caption *Husband Still Missing* underneath it. She noticed Charlie walking in, his eyes looking bloodshot.

"Morning, Charlie. I've got some eggs started, does that sound good?"

Charlie agreed and thanked her. She asked about his eyes; he said thinking of Vivian kept him up. It wasn't a complete lie, except what really kept him up was Mr. Jones—that wasn't the kind of memory that was easy to forget.

Charlie set down his glass of milk and plate of eggs on the brown kitchen table before seeing Kate storm in the kitchen. She snatched some orange juice and sat down with her phone still in hand. Clare and Charlie exchanged looks.

"Someone is framing Michelle for killing Vivian!" Kate finally shouted. Charlie set down his fork and wandered if he heard right.

"What? Did they find evidence pointing to her or something?" Charlie said.

If Michelle killed Vivian, which Charlie doubted, what did the knife at Meredith's house mean?

"Of course not. Someone lied to the cops, saying they found her putting something in Vivian's drink."

Saying it aloud made Kate realize how ridiculous that was. Who would come up with such a dumb story, and why would the cops believe that?

"I guess the police have nothing else to go off of," Clare said.

Kate rolled her eyes in a that-didn't-help-at-all manner.

"I'm sure they will figure it out."

"They didn't figure out what happened to dad," Kate mumbled to herself so quietly Charlie—sitting next to her—didn't hear.

CJ began to cry. Clare set down her plate and took one more sip of coffee before walking to the crib in the other room. Kate leaned in closer to Charlie, almost whispering.

"She said she's been accused of killing and hiding Mr. Jones somewhere, too. I can't let this happen to my friend, Charlie."

They mumbled a few more sentences before deciding to visit Meredith again. Kate must have rubbed off on Charlie, because he suggested recording the conversation between them. *That* could be the true evidence Kate wanted from Meredith.

Then they talked about their father.

"Do you think the same person who killed Vivian also killed dad?"

"So you think he's dead, for sure?" Kate asked.

Kate had a feeling that someday her father would walk through the front door again. Something about it just didn't feel right—the police had shed no light on where her father was killed.

"I just figured," Charlie said.

Kate explained her theory. "Crazy thought, I know. Forget it," she said, looking at her glass.

The one person who knew what happened to Vivian stood by their dark brown desk, smiling at pictures of Michelle. They especially liked the one of her laughing outside of Vivian's house the night of the party, laughing and walking with a boy. She had her phone in one hand and a red cup in the other.

They took the pictures of her and threw them in the trashcan next to the desk, which contained a red cup and a couple of white pearls. A lit match sent the contents into flames, illuminating the dark, hidden house.

Chapter 14: No Dead Body Here, That's For Sure

"I need to see Michelle," Kate said, dangling her car keys from her finger.

She figured it would better to see her alone, so she told Charlie no to coming with her.

She opened the garage door and found a quarter lying on the floor next to a pool of oil. *If this lands on heads, I will find out who killed Vivian and become a hero.* She flipped the coin; it landed on heads and she kept the coin in her palm. Clare met Charlie's stare in the hallway. She wore two gardening gloves.

"What are you doing?" Charlie asked.

Clare explained once more how gardening took her mind off of things. Charlie shrugged but it was when she stepped outside that Charlie realized why this was so bad: Clare could not find out about Mr. Jones.

Charlie ran after her, blocking her way.

"Yes?" Clare asked with an attitude.

Charlie froze. He needed Kate. She was the good liar.

Kate sat at a red light with the music blasting. She viewed her mirror to check her lipstick. There was a black smudge in the corner covering up her eye. She swiped across the stain with her thumb, but it wouldn't come off. She added some saliva to it, but it stayed. Her attention broke when cars behind beeping after the light had turned green for several seconds, and she pressed the gas pedal.

"Charlie what are you doing?" Clare asked, this time more firm.

Before he could answer she shoved his hand out of the way. Clare sat in the front yard, by the bushes outside of Kate's room—they were fine, for now. Charlie dialed Kate on the home phone, not knowing what else to do.

Kate's phone—on silent—lit up inside of her closed purse. She pulled into the driveway to a red brink house. She was forced to enter through the backdoor—several reporters occupied the front door. Michelle had given her an extra key.

"Michelle?" she said as she walked into a kitchen full of dishes in the sink. She walked up the carpeted steps to a narrow hallway with a red rug along it, saying her name once more.

"How'd you get in?" a girl said, opening a bedroom door and holding a tissue.

Kate held up the key. Michelle smiled at her, and motioned for her to enter the bedroom. Michelle told her a lot of people hated her, and it was a matter of time before someone did someone like this to her. She definitely wasn't the nicest person in town, but she wasn't a killer either—that's the one thing she could remember from the party. She got pretty hammered with whatever boy she was with, she claimed.

"Chances are whoever is framing me isn't even the killer—just someone truing to screw me."

"Or cover up for the real killer," Kate said.

Michelle nodded.

"Framing me for Vivian's murder is one thing, but who the hell am I supposed to know where her husband left to? I could care less, honestly."

Kate's throat dried. She played with the zipper on her purse.

"Aren't you going to answer that?" Michelle asked, seeing her phone light up as Kate opened the zipper.

There were four missed calls from the house. That could either mean her mother was furious, or Charlie needed her—bad.

"Sorry, I need to go."

"Everything okay?" Michelle asked.

"Yeah, I just need to get home."

"Pray that nothing happens to me, Kate," Michelle said, with a surprisingly straight face.

Michelle had never said anything like that before. Kate stared back at her, waiting to make some joke—but nothing. Kate squeezed her phone and patted Michelle's hand.

"I'll call you later," she said, ignoring Michelle's comment.

Outside Kate noticed something on her car. It appeared to be a black stain, but also looked like someone scratched the paint—with black nails? Charlie rejoiced when he saw Kate's car pulling into the driveway. She saw mom making her way through the yard and closer to the patch behind the house where their horrible memory sat six feet under—or at least however deep they were able to dig. Kate gave him a we-have-to-stop-her look.

"Mom, don't you think you could put a little more over here?"

Kate pointed towards the front door. She figured Clare would see right through her, but after a few moments Clare agreed.

"You're right. I think I'll add more around here then make a beautiful path around to the backyard in the next couple of days."

Charlie was surprised there wasn't an overwhelming smell of death around the yard. It had only been about two days, and Charlie obviously had no clue when a body started to smell. He just counting his blessings Clare didn't smell anything. The truth would come out sooner than later, Charlie's mind told him. He had no idea what Clare might do to them when she found out. They saw Clare looking noticeably uncomfortable with them standing and staring right at her, so Kate pulled him inside.

"Maybe we just tell her," Charlie blurted, Kate's fingers still pinching Charlie's blue shirt.

Kate was silent for a moment, looking straight out of the front door. Charlie looked back, not sure what to look at.

"What's wrong?" he asked.

"Did you see her?"

Charlie looked back once more, seeing nothing but an empty road. He shot her a confused look.

"Meredith. I just saw her looking out of her window. She saw me then closed the curtains. What is she spying on us for?"

Charlie sat, thinking. What *had* the woman been so interested in them for? There was only one way to find out, Kate figured. Clare slipped back through the door, a shovel broken into two pieces in her hand.

"Ten minutes out there and this cheap thing already broke," she said, throwing it in the trash.

Kate approached her, lying about seeing Michelle again. She told her mother she hadn't been home last time Kate checked.

"Charlie is going, too?"

"She needs as much support as possible right now, Mom," she answered back.

Clare agreed and told them to be careful. Kate grabbed her keys and peeked inside her purse, seeing the knife still wrapped in there. She kept it in there, just in case she needed it.

Chapter 15: The Interrogation Room

Kate knocked on the door, the wood scraping against her bony knuckles. Charlie rubbed his shoe against the splinter-filled wood, nervous about their encounter with the woman again. She must have been annoyed with them by now. They waited a moment before Meredith unlocked three sets of locks on the door and looked at them.

"Hey kids, glad you were able to come visit me again. We never got to finish our chat," she said.

Charlie never heard someone talk the way she did. It was strange; she reminded him of someone, but if he told Kate she would think he was crazy. Before looking at her face, he noticed the white pearl necklace he saw earlier missing from her neck. Of course, she wouldn't wear the same thing everyday, but he noticed her holding onto it the other day. It seemed special to her.

"I liked that white necklace you wore the other day," Charlie said, reaching out his hand to a bottle of lemonade Meredith said she made. He just couldn't see how she would be capable of killing someone—she seemed too innocent. She also handed Kate a glass too, a darker liquid of some sort like that still looked like lemonade.

"You know I loved it too. The weirdest thing happened: I was just at the grocery store yesterday and someone came up and snatched it behind me. By the time I turned around they were gone. I figured it wasn't worth making a fuss over when I could just get another."

Charlie shot her a smile, and then Kate touched his leg, signaling for him to shut up so she could talk.

"Could I ask you a question?" Kate asked.

Meredith shrugged at her, her skin looking suddenly paler.

Kate bluntly asked her how she knew Vivian. Charlie could tell the way Meredith looked at Kate she didn't like her as much as she liked him. He liked her too, in an odd way.

"A lot happens even when you're gone for a short amount of time, sweetie. Friendships were made and broken," she replied, staring at Kate's drink, which she had merely taken a sip of.

You broke my mom's friendship with Vivian by killing her, Kate thought.

Meredith turned to Charlie, wondering if he had anything to ask.

He took a sip of lemonade, his eyes wandering around the room before stopping on a Bible.

"Do you read that?" he wondered.

He never saw anyone read or follow a Bible. He figured everyone used it as a decoration and something to make you look like a person, like his family did. Thinking about it made Charlie realize they weren't that great after all—considering there was a corpse in their backyard and they were crazy enough to be involved in a murder case.

"Of course I do! It's the best weapon I got...obviously I'm not that strong on my own considering I let someone snatch that necklace off of me."

That's it. She's no longer on the suspect list, Charlie thought to himself. He was not going to allow Kate to frame this innocent older woman who just sits and reads the Bible all day.

"You can see the pages look like they've been through war. I feel like that sometimes myself, too," she said.

Kate wasn't going to wait any longer. "I saw you looking at us out of your window just before we came over here."

Meredith shifted in her seat, supporting her head with her hand.

"Those flowers your mother had were too pretty not to look."

"She loves gardening," Charlie added.

"Why did you leave Vivian's party so early?" Kate fired back.

Meredith shrugged and claimed she did not remember because it wasn't important. *Of course it was important,* Kate wanted to yell at her. The woman's voice lowered and her volume declined.

"Sounds like your interrogating me. Not much of a chitchat if you ask me."

Kate told her this was her way of getting to know her better, and jogging her memory of her.

"Well you've got everything backwards. Now the person to learn more about is what's-his-face across the street."

They never thought they would hear something like that out of her mouth. She gazed across the room, daydreaming of whatever man she was referring to.

"He keeps a house key buried under the mulch in the flower pot next his front door. Apparently using it to surprise him when he gets home doesn't exactly attract the right attention from him."

She must have been talking about that man Charlie saw at the party—who was noticeably many years younger than Meredith.

"How do you know he keeps his key there?" Charlie asked curiously.

"I don't have much more to do than to watch people," she said, lifting her shoulders and smiling like it was obvious.

The conversation paused. Charlie set his empty glass on the coffee table in front of him.

"How about I ask you kids something? Have you been questioned or anything by the police yet? Anything?"

Charlie shook his head, swallowing a lump in his throat.

"Huh. Interesting," she said, pulling her lip to the side.

"Have you?" Kate said in a more stern tone.

"That does seem like something even I would remember, doesn't it?" she said with a chuckle.

Then Meredith looked outside at the cloudy sky, and sat up from the chair.

"You kids better get home before this storm hits. I know it's going to hit hard, that's for sure. I need to get back to my reading for the day, anyway. I have to keep the good part of me alive and well."

She pointed towards the door, her hand on Kate's back guiding her out. With Kate's back turned, the woman turned to Charlie, dropping something light in his pocket. She bent down and pressed her mouth against his ear, her gaze still on Kate.

"Be careful about that one—both of them—there's a lot of trouble out there and you don't want to get burnt in it. She doesn't end well."

Charlie looked up at her with a confused look but almost nodded his head at her, also.

"Come on Charlie!"

He waved a small goodbye to her, and she smiled. On the walk home they discussed their conversation. Charlie argued no woman that devoted to the Bible, and innocently lonely, would be capable of murder. Kate disagreed.

"Why exactly do you want to do all of this? What's the point? We are just kids," Charlie said.

"I already told you. Imagine what life will be for us if we are the ones who figure this all out."

"All I care about is being able to sleep once I know who killed dad and possibly Vivian too," he said.

He looked at the man's house Meredith told them about.

"Besides, I think he's a closer guess than Meredith. Things don't add up with her, but he's definitely weird. I remember him at the party staring right at me, and then looking at the punch bowl. He looked weird, almost like he was regretting something."

"Okay Charlie you sound ridiculous."

The two were quiet the rest of the way. Charlie opened the garage door and entered the home. He reached in his pocket and made his way to his room, locking the door. Inside was a wrinkled, aged note from Meredith folded in half. He took a breath and read it:

Chapter 16: Kate Is Road Kill

By nightfall, Clare sat wrapped in a fuzzy blanket on the couch with a box of chocolate in her hand. Night was when thoughts of Vivian hit her the hardest. She played every memory of them together in her head. The doorbell rung, playing much louder in Clare's ears. She made her way, chocolate smeared on the corner of her lip.

A tall man, presumably in his twenties, stood at the door. He ran his hand through his dark brown hair, and then smiled at Clare.

"Are you Clare Stillman?"

"Yes, why?"

"My name is Jason Claremen. I was Vivian's cousin. I'm moving back for obvious reasons. I used to live here, with Vivian, though."

Clare examined the young man.

"How long has it been since you moved away?" she asked.

He chucked. "I'll tell you for a glass of water," he said.

She stepped aside, making room for him to enter.

"It hasn't been long—just enough time to finish some business. I'm looking at this as a blessing, though."

Clare stopped pouring the glass of water, looking at him like he was crazy.

"You mean what happened to Vivian?"

He stepped back and put his hand over his heart, realizing how it must have sounded.

"No, I didn't mean it like that. I'm sorry—I just think my family might accept me now," he said.

Clare asked him what he meant, and more about his family. A drunk driver had killed his parents, and Vivian had taken him in.

"I'm fine now, but it never leaves you, you know?"

Clare nodded and crossed her legs.

"Vivian talked about you all the time. You were the only one she trusted," he added.

She smiled at him, taking a sip from her glass, those thoughts of Vivian swarming inside her head again.

After about five seconds, Kate ran to the door, hearing a knock. Two police officers stood in all black uniforms—unusually dark—, showing her their badges.

"Are you Kate Stillman?" one of them asked.

Kate nodded and he told her she would need to answer some questions.

"About what?"

"You were at Vivian Jones' party the other night, correct?"

"Well, I–"

"It will only be a couple of minutes," he promised.

"So why didn't I ever see you at Vivian's?" Clare asked.

"She hid me, she thought it would be bad for me to associate with her friends, in case I became violent. She wanted to keep her reputation clean."

Clare offered her apologies.

"I'll get out of your way. Thank you," he said, wiping off his seat after standing.

"For what?"

Jason told her she was the only one who opened her door for him.

"You hit one kid making fun of your dead mom and suddenly you're a killer never to be seen with in town."

They took their glasses to the sink, and Clare saw the policemen by the front door. Jason awkwardly slid by them, waving back at Clare one last time.

"Is there some kind of problem officers?"

"We are going to need talk to Kate a little, ask her some questions. Just protocol," the man said.

Protocol? Clare looked at him like he was nuts. She explained everyone had already been questioned at the party.

"Not her," he said strictly.

Kate couldn't help but wander why they hadn't asked for Charlie, as well. He was with her that night, after all. The cops led Kate into her room, leaving Clare outside.

"Can you tell me why you weren't there when we came and questioned everyone that night?"

Kate took a long breath, knowing she would be doing a lot of lying in a short amount of time. "Well my brother CJ was crying and tired, and I went to put him to sleep and let Charlie stay with him for the night. And I was going to leave before that anyway because I forgot my purse."

Without a reply, the man shot another question, this time about a red earring.

"A red earring?" Kate asked.

"Yes. We were sent anonymously a red earring with a tip that it was linked to Mrs. Jones' death, and is being treated as evidence as we look for suspects. It was found next to her body.

Kate began to hear her heartbeat through her ears, and feel blood pumping through her thin veins.

"Yeah, I'm not sure what you're talking about. I don't know who would send that."

"Interesting—because we were also sent this," he said, pulling out a bag with a small photo on it. The photo was of Kate, her earring clearly visible. She hovered over somebody as she held her hand over his or her mouth. Of course, Kate knew that was Charlie, but the picture was blurry and the angle made it nearly impossible to reveal that. Kate muttered something but there was no getting out of this—the photo was proof enough.

"You don't need to say anything else right now. I think we need to continue this at the station."

Kate, too stunned to respond, followed the men as they headed towards the front door again. Clare met her fearful eye. The men explained they needed Kate to come with them to the station, alone. She wasn't a cop, but it didn't' seem like that was necessary for them to do; they hadn't done anything like that with anyone else after the party. She shot her daughter an it-will-be-okay nod and saw her being lead outside the door.

The men guided Kate's head into the car and shut the door. Kate's hands shook as she played the future conversation with the men in her head. Would she be framed for killing Vivian? Who the hell took and sent a picture of her to the cops? She suddenly thought of Michelle. She was being framed, too. That's what didn't make sense—who would frame two people, and what kind of evidence had there been on Michelle? Kate wondered if she would see her there at the station, being further questioned.

The driver slammed the brakes at a stop sign at the end of the neighborhood, thrusting Kate's body forward. She eyed the photo of her in the front seat. It made her look so...*guilty* somehow. She noticed in the bottom left corner—where the man's finger had covered when he showed it to her—a black smear that looked sort of like nail polish, but not quite. The man turned on his signal and began his right turn onto the road.

"Shit," he muttered.

Kate understood. She looked to the left at the accelerating black SUV zooming towards them. It had come out of nowhere. The cop swerved the steering wheel and cussed several more times, the other one holding onto his hat and the seat belt. All in an instant nothing else mattered to Kate—not being framed, the murder case, nothing. She was going to die.

Chapter 17: The Body Count Rises

Kate's head smashed the top of the vehicle as the SUV smashed its side, causing it to roll on its side then flipped upside down in the middle of the road, the black SUV now seemingly out of sight. The car seemed to be driving itself, as if it was hiding in the trees, and then sped at them with the help of a remote controller. The explosion of the airbags echoed in Kate's ears, making her believe she was somehow still alive—even considering the speed at which the SUV hit them. She couldn't say the same for the police officers, who sat breathless with glass piercing their skin. All the remaining energy in her body pushed herself out of the car, her skin tingling from glass pricking her arms and legs.

Something tingled her skin more, though. Once she stumbled back on her feet, she turned towards the area where the SUV had somehow appeared, and there stood Meredith with a concerned look smeared across her thin face.

"We should get you all cleaned up. Let's go back to my place. Are you going to obey me now?" she said.

Kate mimicked her voice as if she was talking to a dog being a trick. Kate didn't have to "obey" anybody. Kate's picked off pieces of glass and rejected her offer, leaving her behind once more. She folded and shoved the picture of herself into her pocket.

"You're welcome," Meredith said.

Clare looked through the peephole, her concern level rising as she saw Kate with several cuts and what looked like glass stuck in her skin. She opened the door, and Kate walked the best she could, her arms noticeably shaking.

"Honey what happened?" she said.

Kate's throat still felt raw and she looked down at her cuts, shaking her head back and fourth. She sniffled and held back tears while her mother brought her inside and tried to clean her up.

An hour later, Charlie spit and wiped the toothpaste off of his mouth. As he opened the bathroom door, he noticed Kate slipping out of the front door once more. He could tell it was she from the bracelet she had been wearing. He was far too tired to worry about where she could have possibly gone now, so he hurried to bed instead, lifting his cold sheets over his body.

Michelle sat on her bed. Her eyes were red and her hair greasy. She hadn't slept in days. In her hand was a Book that she placed on the other side of her as she turned the television on. The volume had been left up high, and she jumped at the noisy children's theme song that was on. She lowered the volume enough to hear the squeak of her cracked-open door. She lowered the volume more and turned her head, but nobody entered the room. She hadn't remembered the air conditioning being strong enough to open her door, though.

"Mom?" she said.

She pulled the blankets over her body when her feet dropped in temperature. Her gaze stood on the door. The hallway light that lit up the carpet next to her door shut off. If her mother or father had turned off the light, why hadn't they responded? What was even weirder was the idea that her parents would even *be* home. She had no idea where they would go during the nights—definitely not anywhere caring about her. As Michelle gripped the edge of her blanket with her sweaty fingers, the door squeaked wider—but stopped almost like on cue. She saw what looked like the edge of a man's dark dress shoe, but didn't have more than half a second to look. Michelle belted out a scream and jumped out of her bed, darting for the window. Her body sunk and felt hot and tingly. Something in her feet felt like a thousand needles pricking her in sync. The last thing she heard was the chanting of the children's program.

Chapter 18: Literally A Skeleton In The Closet

Charlie walked into Kate's room, seeing Band-Aids and creams over her numerous cuts. She lifted her head.

"Sorry, I didn't want to wake you up. Mom wanted me to see how you were doing," he said.

She smiled at him and said she was fine.

"Good thing you rested all night."

Kate turned from him.

"Yeah," she said.

"How late was it when you got in?" Charlie asked.

"You were there, weren't you?" she snapped back.

"Right, sorry. It's just crazy how that car flipped. Kate, were they going to accuse you of anything?"

Kate threw off the covers and opened her curtains halfway, the sun blazing on her left cheek.

"I don't know anything anymore, Charlie. It's not like they can't arrest me—or you, for that matter."

Charlie took a step back, looking at the ground.

"I know. We can't keep what we did a secret forever," he said.

"Well we are just going to have to try," she said before leaving the room.

Her mother checked on her and fed her two eggs with a pancake on the side. She smiled; looking at Kate's cuts and bruises which seemed remarkably better. After breakfast, Kate heard her phone vibrating. She looked at the message that popped on the screen, and attempted to remain calm. She offered to go get some more Band-Aids and ointments.

"Honey I'll do all of that. Besides, how are you ready to be back on the road?" Clare asked.

"I have to do it at some point," Clare said, reaching for her car keys.

She glanced at her phone one more time. The message was from Michelle: *Come over. I know who killed Vivian.* It seemed like forever before she finally pulled into Michelle's driveway, her hands sweating against the leather steering wheel. How had Michelle figured it out? And why hadn't she called Kate instead of texted her? That was something that deserved a phone call. She shut the door and grabbed her spare key as she walked to the back of the house. The mess inside the kitchen was not hard to miss. Plates were cracked, the sink was flooded, and the chairs were on their side.

"Michelle?" she called out.

Walking up the carpeted stairs, she noticed a black mark that looked like a foot print—way too big to be from Michelle.

"Michelle? You here?"

Finally she walked towards Michelle's room, only to hear nothing. The door was cracked, and she pushed it open. The room was empty. On the unmade-bed was an un-topped highlighter on top of a Bible. The television was turned to a televised church service, but she didn't pay attention to that.

Kate pulled out her phone, glanced at Michelle's message once more, and called her. She waited a minute, before hearing Michelle's ringtone—coming from the closet. Before thinking, she lifted the handle of the closet, immediately dropping her phone. Michelle's lifeless body stared back at Kate with open eyes. Her hair fell across her face, and there were two smears on her neck that looked as if someone wiped black nail polish across her. Had someone murdered Michelle because of what she found out? Did that mean she had *just* been murdered—right after she sent that text to Kate? She couldn't think anymore. As soon as she saw the image her body fell back enough for her elbow to fall on top the Bible on the bed, but she didn't care.

At home, Clare frowned at the sight of her garden. It had been nowhere near as good as it used to be. Plants that usually blossomed hadn't shown any sign of life whatsoever, and even the grass began to die. She looked for the hose for several minutes, finding it in the backyard. Heading back to the front of the home, her foot tripped against a small shovel stuck in the ground. She didn't remember doing any gardening there. She pulled the shovel out, seeing a black ribbon attached to it. The ribbon was at least three or four feet long. She tugged the ribbon until it began harder to pull. The ribbon was caught on something. Clare got up from her knees and slowly stood as she yanked the ribbon, wondering what could possibly make it this heavy.

There was plenty of mulch covering the bottom of the ribbon, some which was clearing out of the way. She tugged one more time—regretting that she did.

Charlie heard his mother yell out. He looked out the window seeing her lying on the ground and quickly ran outside. Kate, who hardly had strength to press the gas pedal, pulled in and saw Charlie headed towards the backyard. Charlie looked at whatever could cause Clare to scream like that, and instantly his face turned pale. Kate wiped her eyes and made her way there, too. At the sight the warm dizzying feeling of vomit turned up into her esophagus, and her knees collapsed. In front of them sat something far worse than having Mr. Jones' body discovered by Clare—Michelle's rotting body with a black ribbon tied around her neck.

Out of his blurry eyes, Charlie made out a figure walking towards them to be Jason, wearing a dark jacket and torn blue jeans.

"Oh, there you are. I thought you weren't home, Clare."

It was as if he didn't have eyes, or any human emotion. He ignored the fact that they were standing over a dead body, devastated. Each of them ignored him until he wandered away. Clare alerted the police, and Charlie couldn't help but think his backyard was beginning to turn into a cemetery.

CHAPTER 19: KILLER DISCOVERY

Hours after they discovered the body, and police questioned them, Kate had so many unanswered questions. How the hell had Michelle's dead body move and bury itself? If Clare had been gardening long before she got there, she would have seen someone carrying and burying the body. It was like some supernatural force had swept Michelle away. What Charlie eyed on top of all the mess was Meredith's home, which had caution tape around the front, surrounding huge chunks of broken glass. Two windows had been severally smashed. Kate grabbed his attention and pulled it towards the police officers continuing to inspect the yard, dangerously close to Mr. Jones' body. It was like loud heartbeats every time their feet smacked the ground once more, inching closer to the discover that would put them in jail. Of course, Charlie couldn't think of a way they could pin the murder on them, but he reminded himself how dumb that sounded. There would be nothing they could say to remedy the situation. Clare was tied up with the officers, and Kate had gone in for a moment to prevent from vomiting again. Charlie, his conscious telling him he shouldn't, left for Meredith's house. Out of the corner of her eye, Kate could make out a figure that looked like Charlie going to Meredith's without her; but, before she could follow him, Jason appeared once more at the front door.

Before his eyes noticed Kate, she overheard the end of the phone call he made. All she could make out was, "Those days are over, okay? People change, you know," before he hung up and noticed her. Kate didn't care much for what she heard, considering only Clare had actually talked to him and the image of Michelle's dead body took up all the extra room in her brain.

"You okay?" he asked, her red eyes staring at him.

She wanted nothing to do with this idiot that wasn't even sensitive enough to notice the pain she was enduring.

"Who are you?" Kate snapped back.

Jason didn't move, but reached out his arm towards Kate.

"I know what losing someone is like. I'm Vivian's cousin," he said with a noticeably sterner tone.

"Oh," Kate mumbled while looking at the ground below her.

All in a second, she carried more respect for Jason. Maybe he had an idea of how she was feeling, but wasn't good at expressing that.

"Got a second?" he said while motioning for the two to sit.

The familiar sound of squeaky wooden steps filled Charlie's ears as he approached Meredith's door, inspecting the ground for any pieces of glass that might have made their way towards the entrance. He stared at the yellow caution tape surrounding the portion of the yard to the right of the front door enclosing fallen glass pieces. The broken windows now had bags and tape on them, and Charlie's spine felt a tingle when the thought of sleeping without real windows when an alleged murderer was out there got to him. His gaze drifted the windows after he heard a branch snap—then footprints. At least he thought they were footprints—they sure sounded like them. The door locks loosened and Meredith pushed it open, even though Charlie had not yet knocked. She probably was looking outside even more now, since she needed to be extra careful with those windows. The tape kept the wind out, but didn't have a chance against someone sneaking through them in the middle of the night. Charlie started to feel sorry for Meredith, and his stomach turned at the thought of something happening to her.

"Could I come in?"

A faint smile formed across her thin lips and she opened the wider.

"I saw the tape and the windows, and wanted to see if you were okay. And I didn't know if they questioned you or anyone else for what happened at our place."

She shot him a confused look, and asked him what had happened at his house. He was surprised she didn't know, with all the time she spent looking outside.

"A body was buried in our backyard," he said.

The instant the last word rolled off of his tongue, Charlie realized how it sounded—and dreaded her response.

"You mean the one..."

"No. It was a girl, one of Kate's friends," he said, stopping her halfway.

*She **did** remember seeing us,* Charlie thought. What other body could she have referred to other than Mr. Jones'? Why did she lie to them?

"I'm so sorry, but that's not what the police came here for. Someone broke in."

Charlie apologized in return and shot her a look of sympathy.

"Even with all the things I see I have no idea who it was. I figured it might have been him, hopefully," she said, pointing to the house down the street belonging to the man Charlie had suspicious of at the party.

"He might have wanted his knife back, except my clumsy self lost it," she said.

Charlie's eyes bulged.

"Which knife?"

"Oh just something I found while he was gone, hoping he'd come over here to see if I had seen it. Kind of a dumb idea, I suppose," she said

Before Charlie had the chance to talk about the knife more, Meredith asked to change the subject.

"Well, do you feel safe with only that tape covering your windows?"

"Even if someone comes, at least I won't be so lonely," she responded.

She put her hand on his knee as they sat. Her touch was warm, warmer than he anticipated.

"That's a weird way of looking at things," Charlie responded.

"As far as I'm concerned, I'll be fine, as long as that girl doesn't come walking through those windows," Meredith said, fear stirring in her eyes.

"Kate?" Charlie said, questioning himself why he blurted that out.

He knew she hadn't been too fond of Kate, but that sounded much harsher than he thought Meredith could sound.

"Heavens no. That little girl, whatever her name is. Story is she's possessed, or possesses other people, I don't know. Heard she makes people do all kinds of crazy stuff. I've never actually seen her, but definitely heard an earful."

"Do you believe 'the story'?" he asked.

"A rumor is a rumor, but I don't know. Who knows what kind of evil exists in our world today," she said.

Meredith licked her bottom, dry lip.

"Maybe this psychopath killing innocent people had a small encounter with her," she continued.

Charlie shifted awkwardly in his seat. His mind shifted, as well. On one hand, he regretted making their conversation dive this deep, but he was glad he got the information about the knife. Now he really knew who killed Vivian.

Chapter 20: Waiting Outside Your Window

Kate and Jason's conversation continued, along with occasional laughs from the two.

"Thank you," Kate said with a flirty smile.

"For what?" "For making my day a lot better," she replied.

"Glad I could help. I'm glad I met you. Sorry again about earlier, I wasn't thinking at all. Tell your mom I said hi."

Kate nodded and sat up.

"I'll see you around?"

"Sounds good. Goodnight," Jason said as he walked past Kate to the front door, her nose catching the sweet smell of his cologne.

"I need to get back home. Sorry if I bothered you," Charlie said.

Meredith sat up and fixed her hair. As Charlie's feet approached the door, she grabbed his shoulder, stopping him.

"Let me tell you one more thing. Be careful about that sister of yours. You never really know the people close to you, just remember that. Okay?"

Her grip loosened and Charlie looked at her, now walking towards her Bible on the coffee table. He tried to mumble something back, but she began reading and he just turned back, feeling more confused than ever. He shut the door behind him, perplexed at how bad of a person Kate could possibly be—in Meredith's eyes. Had she known something about Kate that Charlie didn't? As soon as Charlie's feet hit his driveway, he could make out Kate staring behind the front door, waiting for his explanation.

"We need to talk," he told her.

She shut the door closed.

"What were you over there for?"

"She didn't kill Vivian," Charlie said, almost in an I-told-you manner.

"How do you know?"

Charlie opened his mouth, but Clare entered and interrupted.

"It's getting late, guys. Make sure you have clothes picked out for the...funeral. Where have you been?"

"We talked with Jason for a while."

"Oh, Vivian's cousin? That's good. Maybe we can sit with him tomorrow, he seems lonely and abandoned by Vivian's family."

They all kissed goodnight and Kate followed behind Charlie to his room.

"The knife we found belongs to that weird guy across the street. She said she found it at his place when she was there, and took it. I know it sounds dumb, but I know she was telling the truth. We've been looking at the wrong person," Charlie said, having to take several large breaths to tell Kate all of it.

"Why would he have the knife? Mrs. Jones didn't have a puncture wound. There was no trace of any weapon...she just collapsed. But obviously someone killed her."

Charlie couldn't help but think Kate was the one so convinced the knife killed her.

"Even if she didn't kill anyone, don't go there alone, got it?"

"Okay, fine. I felt sorry for her, someone tried to break in and broke her windows."

Kate yawned and didn't respond.

"The person who killed Vivian—and Michelle, for that matter—could have killed Meredith too," Charlie said sincerely.

Kate barely nodded her head but went for the door still.

"I know, I know. Let's get some sleep. It's been a long day."

"Yeah, goodnight," he said.

Outside, the bushes shook and branches snapped. A pair of (rather small) feet ran through the night, and pounded against the pillow of grass below. Breathing became more difficult as the shadow ran in the chilly hours that easily dried up their throat and lungs. Their breath looked like the fog surrounding the neighborhood as the figure exhaled. Soon the ground went still, and the only noise came from the strong wind, which shook the tape of Meredith's windows, where the feet halted.

CHAPTER 21: TENSION

Kate ran the comb through her thick hair once more before exiting the car, stepping up the church steps. Immediately she, along with Charlie and Clare, were hugging and talking with Vivian's family, who looked miserable but attempting to hold it together. Sharon, Vivian's mother, had her red hair put into a bun and wore a fitting, long black dress. She squeezed Clare's shoulders and pulled her mouth closer to her right ear.

"Thank you so much for coming," Sharon said.

"Of course I came, don't be silly. How are you holding up?"

"I'm getting there. I just can't believe she's..."

The woman's eyes started to water. Clare wrapped her arms around her once more. In the corner of Clare's eye stood Jason in a black shirt and black dress pants. To Clare's surprise, he was not dressed in a complete suit—a little inappropriate, in her eyes. Clare waved, shining a smile at him as well, which was something Sharon did not do. Clare only got a glance of Sharon's reaction, but it look like she frowned when she saw him. Noticing Sharon's disappointment, he walked awkwardly past the two.

"Why didn't you invite him to stay with us?"

"It's bad enough I'm at my daughters funeral, isn't it Clare?" said Sharon.

Clare's logic told her to shut up, so she opened the church door for them and noticed the burning candles and the flood of black suits and dresses that walked near her. As she tried to find a seat, the rest of Vivian's family motioned for Clare, Kate, and Charlie to sit with them up front. As they sat down, Clare noticed Jason sitting by himself, looking as rejected as he said he was that night with her. Moments before the service began, Charlie turned his head to see the man from the party—and now the real owner of the engraved knife—staring right at him and Kate.

"Who is that?" Clare whispered in Sharon's ear.

An older woman, dressed in all black, sat at the end of pew, tissues in hand.

"Ashley. Nathan's mother," she said.

Clare's head lowered and she shook her head slightly.

"Poor thing."

"It's definitely hard on her, not knowing if she will see ever see her son again."

Clare asked if the police had any idea where he might be, but there were no leads. He had just...*disappeared.*

At the end of the service, Kate caught Jason, and Charlie's eyes fell on an icon of Jesus towards the front door. He felt different being in a church, better than usual, especially with all the chaos that happening. He had only been in a church a few times, mainly for weddings and other ceremonies, though. Kate and Clare hadn't cared much for it. They enjoyed their extra sleep on Sunday mornings. Next, his eyes gazed on a boy struggling to get his wheelchair through the front door. He, in a second, recognized the boy, and had seen him at Vivian's party. He glanced at the icon on the wall once more, and then approached the boy.

"Henry?"

The boy turned his head, but didn't crack a smile at the sight of Charlie.

"Hey, Charlie," the boy said, turning his head.

"Look, I know you aren't happy to see me. And I know you thought you would never have to see me again. But I just wanted to apologize...for everything. I've changed, or at least I'm changing, I think."

"I'm fine," the boy mumbled.

Charlie had an overwhelming feeling of guilt in his gut. His friends had bullied that boy so badly, making fun of everything about him. Charlie really *was* changing—he usually didn't feel guilty about anything, but that had changed lately.

"Really, Henry. No jokes, no games. I really am sorry, and shouldn't have done any of that stuff to you. My friends and I were stupid and immature, and didn't know what our jokes did to you."

He finally turned to Charlie, a faint smile forming with his lips.

"Well, thank you."

"I know we may never be close, but I wanted you to know how sorry I was for making fun of you all this time, in case I didn't have the chance later."

After a second of confusion over what Charlie meant by not having the chance later, he smiled wider.

"Thank you. It's nice to hear you finally say that. Nobody else has."

Charlie smiled and helped push his chair through the door.

"See you around," said the boy one last time.

Charlie walked out the front door, as it started to drizzle. Someone tapped his right shoulder.

"Oh, hey! Did you just get here?"

"Well, nobody would dare look at me here," Meredith said, taking her hand off his shoulder.

"That's ridiculous," he said.

"That was nice, what you just did."

Charlie smiled and nodded.

"I needed to do it. I've done some bad things in the past," he said.

"Well that's the past. You're different now. I've done things I'm not proud of, too. We all have. Sometimes our bad side gets the best of us. Except that family of yours, especially your sister. Haven't seen much of anything besides her bad side. I'm sorry I keep talking about her like that, but something pretty disturbing happened.

Charlie's eyes focused on her, his heartbeat rising.

"She's the one who broke my windows."

He took a small step back, and didn't realize his mouth was hanging open.

"What?"

"One of the neighbor's security cameras picked her up. Saw the tape myself."

She sounded like someone had lied straight to her face, her voice straining and she looked like she had been betrayed. Even though she wasn't as close to Kate, that had still been someone totally uncalled for. What had Kate been thinking?

"That girl does nothing but bad things, then obsesses over making other people look guilty, probably to cover up all of her crimes."

"Kate wouldn't kill her best friend."

"A sick way of making her look innocent, if you ask me. Now nobody would ever think of her being involved in any of this."

Charlie looked over at Kate talking with Jason.

"I'm glad you could come," he said.

"Of course. It's the least I could do. I can't imagine how you are feeling."

"I could say the same to you, considering what happened to your...well you know."

Kate bit the inside of her lip, thinking of Michelle.

"Why didn't you sit with us, or for your family, for that matter?"

Jason made the lame excuse that there hadn't been enough room, but Kate saw right through that. Maybe he hadn't thought of her the way she began to think of him.

"Well, did the service...help at all?" she said, sounding like an idiot in her mind.

"A little, but it can only do so much."

Kate nodded.

"If you ever need anything..."

"Thank you," he said, giving her a hug.

Sharon and Clare walked out together, and Sharon noticed Jason.

"Aren't you worried about Kate talking with Jason?"

"What's there to be worried about? He's nice."

"Yeah, when there's money involved," she said.

"I don't understand," Clare said.

Their conversation continued in patches. Sharon was greeted and supported by two or three people, then turned to Clare, and that repeated.

"He left home, hardly cared for parents, and comes back to inherit Vivian's money? That guy's nothing but trouble."

"How do you know he didn't leave because he didn't feel wanted?"

"Please, we practically smothered him in our arms. He hit a low point in life by himself, and saw Vivian's wealth as the escape. Just thinking about it makes me sick. Vivian didn't even get the chance to change her will. Who knows what he's capable of."

Clare took a big breath, and looked over at Kate, who giggled and hugged Jason. After a moment, Clare waved goodbye to Sharon after one last. Charlie and Kate told Meredith and Jason bye, and walked towards each other. They noticed a woman pull a man aside and refer to him as Victor, and she greeted him with a smile. Both Kate and Charlie overheard it—the man from the voicemail. Charlie looked at the man once more, realizing he was the one who killed Vivian—in his eyes, of course. He thought harder, his stomach suddenly hurting at the thought of a killer talking, or leaving messages, with his mother.

As he thought of Clare, she pulled both him and Kate closer and headed for the car.

"I met Nathan's mother. Looks like she hasn't slept since the party. It must be unbearable for her."

The two didn't even bother looking at each other. If Kate looked back at Charlie, Clare may have gotten suspicious. They left it at biting their lips and ignoring Clare altogether.

Everyone but Clare made their way into the house. Kate held CJ. Clare attempted to fix the damage done to the garden, but hardly moved. She gradually realized it was a waste of time.

"Well we know his name now," Kate said as she put CJ down.

"Why didn't he talk to mom, if he knows her?"

"No idea. Something still feels weird about him, and what's even weirder is how mom never mentioned him to us."

Clare entered the room with a bath towel in her hand.

"I'm taking a shower, make sure you guys don't wrinkle those clothes," she said.

Part of them said Clare had overheard the last portion of their conversation, but the other part said they had bigger things to worry about.

"We need to go over there, too."

"At his house? Don't you think going over to Meredith's made things more complicated?"

"Charlie, we are getting closer, I just know it. This is the next piece of the puzzle. You told me where Meredith said he hides his key. All we have to do is sneak in when he leaves."

"Wait, you want us to break in? We didn't do that with Meredith," Charlie argued.

Kate's plans seemed to never stop. Charlie didn't feel like getting arrested for murder *and* breaking into the man's house.

"What if this guy is dangerous, Charlie? Yeah that makes it risky to go over to his house, but do you want him to hurt mom?"

"Don't go there, Kate."

"I'm not kidding Charlie, you never know with what's been happening. Please, for mom's sake."

Kate walked to the curtains, noticing how dark his house was kept, even in broad daylight. His car had been parked in the driveway, so it wasn't like he wasn't home. Charlie saw a faint shadow pass through the window, but couldn't truly see the man.

"Let's keep an eye out and go over there when the time's right. *This* could be what could keep us out of jail, Charlie. If he killed Vivian, there will be less of a chance of us being charged for Mr. Jones' death, and I don't think we need to worry about Meredith even remembering seeing us."

Charlie looked at the ground, thinking of what Meredith had said when he told her there was a body found.

"Listen to yourself. You were so convinced Meredith was the killer; now you're set on Victor. It's only a matter of time before we get caught. We can't just obsess over all of this stuff."

After several comebacks by Kate, and refusals by Charlie, Kate stormed out. She watched Victor's house for several hours, glancing to see if his car was missing every once and a while. Finally the lights in the house powered off, and Victor stepped outside and locked the front door. He didn't leave with his car, though. He walked out of the driveway, and made his way down the road. Kate ran to put her shoes on, making noise outside of Charlie's room on purpose. Maybe he had changed his mind. She waited one more moment as she slipped her left Nike sneaker on, but he didn't come out of his room. She made her way across the street, and snuck around the back of his house to make sure nobody would see her. She didn't; however, notice the woman walking her dog near Victor's home who clearly saw Kate. She stopped walking and pulled out her cell phone, but Kate didn't see anything.

Chapter 22: Putting The Pieces Together?

Charlie watched Kate through the blinds, noting she did an impressive job of getting in. She turned on a lamp in what looked like a kitchen. What caught his eyes as he nearly closed the curtains was a figure walking towards the home—it was Victor. He dug around in his pocket as if he left something. After mentally debating with himself, Charlie decided to put on his shoes. Since Kate left her phone in Charlie's room, he sprinted to Victor's home, trying his hardest to beat Victor. He couldn't let Kate go down and be caught like this, he just couldn't. Kate continued to look around the rundown house. The carpet had several stains, and on the kitchen table two wine glasses and two plates.

She made her way to the bathroom, the mirror still foggy and the curtain still wet. Kate began to look through the cabinets in the room, and her jaw dropped. Inside one was a gold earring that she recognized in an instant. It was the exact same one Kate's father had given her for her birthday, the day he died. How had he gotten a hold on this? Kate was scared to touch it, and memories of her father flooded in the back of her brain.

Victor continued walking, now even closer to his home. A man with baggy shorts and an athletic top took out his earphones and stopped him. Victor smiled at the man and then began a short conversation even though Victor looked desperate to get something from home he forgot.

Kate built up the courage to touch the earring, and put it in her pocket without looking at it again. Outside the bathroom, on a dresser, stood a picture of Clare. *What the hell is with this guy,* Kate thought. It was like this man was screaming he's the killer all over the house with this evidence, in Kate's eyes. Victor finished his conversation and waved to the man, now headed closer to his house. He walked faster than before, looking at his watch. Kate figured the earring and Clare's picture alone was enough for right now, so she headed towards the door. However, yet something else caught her eye. In the trash can in the kitchen was another picture—but not of Clare. It was of Vivian, and had a large crack through the middle, where her lips were. She dared to pick it up, seeing something else wrinkled underneath it. There was an invitation for Vivian's party that was also ripped.

"Bingo," she whispered.

She heard footsteps approaching. The sound of branches and leaves breaking filled her mind. A glimpse of a figure caught her eye, but they were gone. The footsteps sounded closer, and closer. She was too far from the door—she needed to hide. She put the pictures back in the trash bin, and turned off the lights, realizing a second later she probably just showed Victor she was in here by doing that. She hid and ducked below the kitchen island. She held her breath due to her breath being unsteady and making too much noise. She waited for the door to stop squeaking open before looking, and she took a huge sigh. It was Charlie.

"What are you doing?" she said.

Kate startled Charlie since he hadn't seen her, but didn't respond. He walked over to her and motioned for the door. The next sound was Victor's keys, and the two saw the doorknob turning. Charlie wished he hadn't gotten closer to Kate, because now both of them were too far from the door. Charlie grabbed her hand and rushed into a small, cramped closet next to the kitchen. The man walked in, his shoes dress shoes sounding like high heels. Charlie could feel Kate's hot breath on his neck as they crammed into the tiny space. Kate's hand shook, and she regretted coming over here. Charlie was right—she hated that. It was like she was always wrong, even though she was older. Victor noticed and found his phone sitting next to his house phone near the kitchen table, and put it in his pocket. Kate watched through the crack in the closet, and didn't remember seeing his phone anywhere, otherwise she would looked through it for sure. Victor walked towards the closet, making them both hold their breath. Except he stopped just short of the closet to check his reflection in the full-length mirror that hung next to them. They continued watching through the crack, having to squint to see anything. Finally, he walked away and left the house, locking the front door. They both let out huge sighs. Kate opened the closet.

"That was close."

"Yeah, just what I was afraid of," Charlie said.

Kate couldn't help but feel like an idiot, but she *had* found some evidence, possibly.

"Your lucky I came. He would have caught you, for sure."

"Thanks," she mumbled.

"We need to get out of here."

"First, look at what I found."

She started with the earring, not being able to explain much before the risk of crying about her father kicked in, but she tried. Then she guided him to the trashcan.

"That's not a coincidence," said Kate.

Charlie didn't look too interested. For all he knew Kate could have smashed that picture herself before he got there. Overtime he thought about who this killer could be, Kate ruined it for him. Now that she was obsessed with exposing Victor as the killer, he didn't think the same anymore. But something about him was still weird—he could just feel it. At this point his attitude was whatever happens, unlike Kate.

"Come on, you know this is weird."

"Yeah, it's weird, but that doesn't mean he killed her. And there's no broken picture of Michelle," he pointed out.

"Well obviously he and Vivian weren't great friends. Something must have happened between them. That wouldn't explain why she would invite him to the party, though."

"Okay, whatever. I don't see any other pictures, let's just leave before we get caught again."

Kate was quick to show him the pictures of Clare, trying everything to convince him. It looked like he had finally given in, at least a little.

"Pictures of mom?" he said, raising his eyebrows.

Now he felt like Victor was weirder than he thought, and he felt scared. Kate suddenly realized a possible explanation.

"Think about it, Charlie. He only has pictures of women- one of which he probably killed. Both people that were murdered have been women."

That *did* sound convincing. Kate went and grabbed both the invitation and the cracked picture from the trash.

"Are you crazy? Now he will know someone was in here."

"Not if we prove he killed Vivian and Michelle first."

Charlie wasn't going to win this battle, he knew that much. He let her be and they closed the back door, sprinting back home.

Chapter 23: You're Seeing a Killer!

Clare sat on the couch at home next to a police officer.

"Thank you for everything. I just wanted to know if you guys had any leads so far. Now, can you tell me more about Jason?"

"Clare, I shouldn't say more than I already have," the police officer said.

"Please, Bill. I need to know who to protect my family from."

He could sense the fear in her voice. He paused for a moment, and made her promise everything he said would be off the record. Besides, Bill had been a friend with the family for quite a while.

"All that sob story stuff about his parents—it's all BS. His parents *are* dead, but he lied about who his parents are."

"Well who are his parents?"

He paused once more, licking his lips.

"Please, Bill."

"Nathan and Vivian are," he said.

She backed up from him and shot a confused look his way.

"No, there's no way," said Clare firmly.

"He's not her cousin. Vivian loved him so much, and did everything for him. All that shit about nobody caring is an act."

"Why didn't I ever see him at Vivian's house?"

"Story is he landed in juvie over and over, then jail, and eventually moved away."

"And I'm guessing he just came back to town?"

"Actually he was just released from prison—I'm not sure why he was there this time—a couple of days before Vivian's party. Rumor is he killed her for her money."

"I didn't even see him there," she argued.

"Nobody did, which makes him more suspicious."

The sound of the door interrupted their conversation. Charlie and Kate walked in, their minds thinking the worst when they saw Bill. Police officers hadn't meant good news lately.

"I should get going," he said.

"Thank you, again."

He shut the door. Kate realized she would need a bigger purse soon with all the things she stuffed in it. She put the things from Victor in the bag, realizing it now had her fingerprints on it.

"Lately I've realized how careful we need to be. We can't trust anyone, and have to be careful about who we talk to," Clare said, mainly directing herself towards Kate.

Charlie nodded his head in agreement, noticing her staring at Kate.

"Is that clear?"

"Yes, okay. Whatever," she said. CJ began crying, and Clare went to his crib.

In the family room, the television blasted. The news was on: WOMAN FOUND DEAD the screen read. Charlie did a trouble take when he noticed the picture next to the caption. *How* was this possible? *This has to be a mistake*, he thought. Kate was equally as shocked, but for a slightly different reason.

"You were right about her," Kate whispered as her gaze stood on the television. The picture of Meredith was one Charlie hadn't seen before, she looked younger and happier. Something about her looked familiar, though. He couldn't place his finger on it, but was too shocked to think further. Meredith was dead. The woman Kate was so hung up on getting arrested was no longer alive. Charlie felt around his pocket, which still held the note Meredith had given him. All of a sudden, Charlie's throat dried. His skin became warmer, and his veins tensed and popped out. He shook his legs in a nervous, angry fashion and looked at the aged carpet below him, becoming furious. What did killing an innocent woman do for anyone? He felt like hitting something. He knew Kate hadn't felt the same way, either. All she did was smash Meredith's windows, nothing beneficial. On the other hand, he was forming a genuine relationship with her. She began to teach him things Clare and Kate never could. He began to feel like a better person with Meredith, even with all that he was guilty of. It was like she had everything he was missing. Now she was gone.

"I didn't even get to say goodbye," he said.

"This is what I'm talking about, Charlie—nobody's safe. And think about it, it's another girl murdered. It's making more and more sense. Maybe Victor had some broken pictures of Meredith, too."

Charlie wanted to smack Kate. He couldn't care less about all of this anymore. All he wanted was to talk with Meredith, just one last time.

"Kate! Charlie!" Clare shouted.

She pounded her feet against the floor and charged for Kate's purse. She tore through it, finding everything from Victor's. Luckily she hid the knife away in her room.

"Where did you get these? Don't think about lying to me. I already know the answer."

Charlie hadn't seen his mother this mad in a while.

"Mom..."

"Lindsey down the street called and said you went into Victor Jenkins's house.

"Mom, I...had to," Kate said.

She thought about ratting out Charlie for being there to, but he was why Victor didn't catch her himself. Clare crossed her arms and waited for a true explanation.

"We think he killed Vivian," she said.

Kate surprised herself as she let that out. Clare looked disgusted. Charlie shrugged when he heard Kate say *we*. He was done with all of this—she was on her own.

"And what makes him so convincing?" Clare asked.

Kate glanced at Charlie, seeing that he was waiting for her to talk. She really was on her own.

"Look at those pictures. He probably hated Vivian. And we found a knife that he probably stole from her, too."

"So that makes him a killer?"

Kate wished once, just once, Clare would listen to her. She was right this time, she could feel it—but reasoning with her mother, or convincing her of anything was close to impossible.

"You can't break into people's houses, Kate. It's up to the police to figure all of this out."

"The police aren't doing anything, Mom. Or they aren't doing things fast enough. Another murder just happened."

Charlie hated to feel sorry for Kate, but he did a little.

"That's true," he said in almost in a whisper.

Kate smiled at him, and then continued arguing with her mother.

"He has pictures of you at his house too, Mom! He's dangerous. Who knows who could be next?"

"This conversation is over. Promise me you won't go over there anymore."

Kate rubbed her cool arm and looked at the ground.

"Kate."

"Okay, I promise," she said, still looking at the ground.

Kate walked to her room, furious that her mother hadn't believed her. Charlie turned off the TV.

Later that night, Charlie knocked on Kate's bedroom door. She opened it, acting surprisingly happier.

"Did you change you mind? Realize I'm right about Victor?" she said in a bragging tone.

Charlie remained still, not cracking a smile.

"What were you trying to accomplish smashing Meredith's windows? Why would you go over there again? Especially after the car accident, which you were lucky you survived. What—were you going to kill her?"

Kate's smile disappeared. How had he found out about that? She took her hand off of the door handle and took a seat on her unmade bed.

"Here we go again. I already got mom's lecture, I don't need another one, Charlie."

She motioned for him to just leave, but he didn't budge.

"I deserve an answer. What could have made that mad? And did you think nobody would see you? I thought you would have learned that lesson by now, Kate."

"Oh my God, Charlie," she said.

He hated when she, or his mother, said that. It sounded so...wrong, disrespectful. But they didn't understand it.

"Finding your best friend's dead body might make you mad enough to smash a window or two."

"That doesn't add up. We saw her body in the backyard after you broke the windows."

"Okay, Charlie. After the accident she just said some stuff to me and I really thought she killed Vivian so I just smashed her window. I wasn't trying to kill her. It was stupid, I know, but she made me so mad that night."

"Well what did she say?"

"It's over with, Charlie. Doesn't matter. But what does is the fact that I saw Michelle's body at her house first, before we found her in the yard. It was like someone—or something—moved her body. Almost like something un-human."

"Why didn't you tell me? Are you sure you didn't imagine that?"

Kate looked at him like he was crazy.

"No I did not imagine it! And don't you think it's right for me to know who killed my best friend?"

"Listen, Kate. We must be doing something wrong. Everyone around *us* is dying. This didn't happen before we came. It's like every time we talk to someone, they are dead the next day."

Kate tried to speak, but Charlie continued.

"Someone has it out for *us*, and they are obviously good at staying hidden. This is what they've wanted all along- for us to get so obsessed with finding them we forget about more important things in our lives. All of this is out of our hands."

He had never spoken like that to her, but she had to admit he made sense. The people that have been murdered were closer to them than anyone else. The lights in the room flickered on and off, and Kate's cell phone chimed. She took a big breath, and walked past Charlie, hitting his shoulder. She walked out of the front door to see Jason waiting outside. She saw him putting something in his pocket, but didn't ask.

"Hey! I didn't catch you at a bad time, did I?" he asked.

"Of course not," she said.

She got a look at his shiny shoes she hadn't seen before.

"Are those new?"

He looked down at them, concern spreading on his face.

"Oh, yeah. I just got them. Figured it was time for new ones. Mine smelled like an old prison."

He gave a genuine-sounding laugh, and so did Kate.

"Ew," she giggled.

She noticed a watch on his right wrist as well.

"New watch, too?"

He smiled awkwardly and covered it with his other hand.

"I thought it might make me feel better. Have you seen the news?"

Kate nodded. Charlie watched their conversation through the blinds.

"What a shame," he said.

He looked down at his watch, while Kate glanced over at Victor's house. He opened his door, a big trash bag in his gloved-hands.

"You okay?"

Victor carefully put the bag into his trash bin, then stared straight at Kate. Jason touched her arm, redirecting her attention.

"Oh, sorry. It's just...he's so weird."

Jason glanced at the man too, now going inside.

"Who is that?

"Victor's his name. I know it's crazy, but I think he..."
Before she could finish, he looked down at his watch, drowning out Kate.

"What'd you say? Sorry."

"His name is Victor. He has creepy pictures of my mom...and Vivian in there."

"What? How do you know that?"

He looked disgusted.

"I broke into his house."

Jason took it as a joke, and laughed.

"Is that a hobby of yours? Have you broken into my place? Seen what I've got hidden in there?" he said playfully.

She tried to laugh back, not quite telling if he was joking or not.

"No, of course not. I just knew something was up with him."

Inside, Victor grabbed his phone and rested it between his shoulder and ear. He took his gloves off, and put them into his empty trash bin.

"Are you sure? Did they tell you? Did *you* tell *them?"* he said through the phone.

He sighed and squeezed the phone.

"Okay, come over. We'll talk it about more. The kids will be fine for a few minutes," he said before ending the call.

Jason looked at the time one final time.

"I better get going. Sorry, I wish I could stay longer," Jason said.

"Where are you going?" Kate said.

"I've got some stuff to take care of. It was good seeing you, again. Bye," he said.

They hugged and he left. Kate, once she got inside, noticed Charlie on the computer.

"What are you doing?"

He stayed silent for several seconds, but finally turned his head.

"Looking up Meredith. I wanted to see if there were any friends, family, or any connections to her. But there's nothing."

"I'm sorry."

"For what?"

"Just...I'm sorry," she said before leaving.

Charlie turned off the computer, and went to the drawer in the living room. He picked up a dusty Bible and took it to his room.

In her room, Kate flipped through a fashion magazine, thinking that would solve her problems. Clare set CJ down in his crib and threw on a pair of jeans. She took everything that Kate had stolen—she made her give it to Clare—and put it in her purse, and then headed to Victor's house.

"Mom, did you take my green tank top?"

Kate waited a moment, not hearing any response.

"Mom?"

She checked her empty bedroom, and then rolled her eyes at Charlie, seeing what he was reading as she passed his room. Just as she was about to go back into her room, she noticed something outside the kitchen window. It was Clare, or at least it looked her. She knocked on Victor's house. On top of other thoughts, Kate thought it was pretty dumb of her mother to leave them alone with all that has happened, even if she was a teenager.

"Oh my God," she said, seeing her mother enter the dim house.

"Mom is with a killer! We have to stop her."

Charlie stopped reading.

"Stop it, Kate."

"How can I, Charlie? Mom's over there with Victor and all you're doing is reading. We have to help her. Please, I promise if I'm wrong about this I won't ask you for anything else ever again.

Charlie looked down and continued reading, then took a sip of water. He could tell she wasn't leaving. Her face was so desperate.

"One more chance, please Charlie," she pleaded.

He looked out the window once more, the lights in Victor's house turning low enough for them to hardly see anything. Finally, he stood up. Kate smiled.

"What exactly are you thinking?"

"I'm ending this, once and for all. And saving mom," she said.

"What if we're too late? Why is the house that dark?"

Kate ignored him and ran to Victor's house—only to find the hidden key missing from the mulch in the flowerpot.

"What now?"

Kate remembered seeing Victor coming out with a shovel one day. He had dug some holes around his yard; she wasn't sure what for though. They went around back, not afraid of getting caught since the blinds were, at this point, closed so nobody could see in or out.

"Kate, you're not going to..."

It was too late. Kate picked up the muddy shovel and thrusted it at the window. Charlie thought about how she had done this to Meredith's home, and how much he missed her. He breathed a sigh of relief when he heard Clare's voice from inside.

"Kate! What have you done? We talked about this!"

Clare and Victor were sitting at the dark brown table, holding a glass of wine each. Clare jumped up in shock.

"Mom, you are with a killer! He has my earring from the day dad died. He killed my best friend, for God's sakes!"

Charlie cringed.

"Kate, stop it right now."

Victor stood up and turned on several lights.

"Listen, I'm no killer," Victor said.

"Take Charlie home right now, Kate."

Kate refused.

"No, not until this man admits what he's done. He killed my best friend Mom, does that mean nothing to you?"

The vein running through Clare's forehead became visible, an easy way of telling how tense she was.

"Okay, fine. Kate, Charlie, sit down. I need to tell you this; maybe it will make you change your minds. Victor and I have been seeing each other for quite a while."

Kate's mouth went dry, and Charlie didn't realize his mouth hanging open.

"*Seeing* each other?" Charlie asked.

"I wanted to tell you."

"Then why didn't you?" Kate snapped back.

Clare didn't say anything, but took a sip of wine.

"Does that have something to do with why we really came back home?"

Victor wanted to try explaining, but he knew how the kids already felt about them. Talking would be pointless.

"The baby that I...lost, belonged to Victor. I didn't know whom to turn to after I lost it. I needed to come back. I needed to tell him in person. That house wasn't doing anything for us, anyway."

Charlie suddenly realized how selfish her mother was. She had never cared about his idea that the house was haunted, and she had lied to him all of this time. It sounded so much like...Kate, not his mother.

"So you were seeing him...while dad was, alive? And he thought it was his baby?"

"I'm so sorry."

"You've been lying to us all this time? Have you known he's a killer? Is that why you wanted us to stop searching—you were scared we would realize it was Victor?"

Kate's voice was powerful and angry. The house felt like it was shaking as she yelled.

"My God, Kate! He didn't kill anyone!"

"How do you explain him having my earrings from the day dad died?"

Kate knew her mother wouldn't be able to answer that, unless she lied of course. She wanted Clare to just give up—her mother knew Victor was the killer and there was nothing to say to make it better. Charlie thought, for half of a second, if his mother had helped Victor at all...*stop it*, he told himself. His own mother would never help a killer—but it seemed like an awful amount of work for one person.

"How about those being a pair he bought me last week? Those weren't the only pairs on the world, Kate."

"That doesn't matter. He still obviously hated Vivian, and killed her."

Looking like he was about to explode, Victor finally spoke.

"Way back, Vivian and I dated. She dumped me the night I was going to purpose. I found those pictures in the attic, and only ripped her invitation because I always saw how happy she was at those parties."

Likely story, Kate thought. Of course he had a script planned for what he would say if he was caught.

"But you still went to the party?" Charlie said.

Kate was surprised Charlie spoke, and figured he was finally convinced enough of Victor to accuse him further.

"Only because your mom wanted me to. And I hadn't seen her since you all left."

"Well you stole a knife from Vivian with her initials on it. Were you planning to use that on her?"

"She gave me that as a gift when we dated. I found it in the rest of the stuff from her."

Victor was acting surprisingly calmer now that he got to get his story—which was total BS, Kate decided—out.

"Come on, what kind of a gift is a knife?" Kate asked.

Now it was official—Victor was lying. The story started to make sense, but Kate knew nobody gave a knife as a gift.

"Wasn't my idea. But how many times have you guys broken in here? That knife's been missing for weeks."

Kate glanced at Charlie, and him at her. Their minds went to Meredith. She had told the truth about finding the knife there.

"Never mind all of this. Kate, Charlie, we are going home. Apologize to Victor."

They mumbled some words, but nothing like an apology. Kate wanted to keep talking, but Clare pushed them both towards the door.

"I'm so sorry for all of this. I'll pay for the window," said Clare.

"Don't worry about it. Focus on them, for now. They need you."

They exchanged looks before she shoved them out the door. Nobody said a word on the walk home.

CHAPTER 24: CHARLIE VS. THE DARKNESS

Thunder pounded in the air as Clare led them inside their house. They spent the first hour home all doing different things: Charlie read The Bible, Kate blasted music and rehearsed what she would tell the police about Victor—she decided by the end of the night she would call and report him as the killer of Vivian, Michelle, and Meredith, and knew she had to have her story straight—and Clare searched her wallet and bank accounts, trying to find a way to pay for Victor's windows. The last thing she wanted to do was see Kate, as awful as it sounded. Never in her life was someone so disrespectful. She went back and fourth, thinking about making Kate pay for the windows.

Clare thought about how the way she would have *liked* to tell them about her and Victor, but there would not have been a good way. The outcome would have been the same. She made a mistake, and had to pay for it.

After finishing a verse, Charlie knocked on Kate's door. He had to wiggle the locked doorknob since he figured she was listening to music and wouldn't hear him.

"Just say it," she said once she opened the door.

"What?"

"I don't know. Something about me messing things up again. I still think he killed them though, Charlie."

"I feel a lot better than I did an hour ago," he said.

"What do you mean?"

I don't know, I just feel like everything will work out."

By the confusion on Kate's face, Charlie decided to jut give up. She didn't understand.

"You must have not been in the same room I was. Our mother had an affair and didn't tell us, and possibly helped Victor kill all of these people. But whatever, Charlie. Shut the door on your way out," she said, too busy thinking of calling the police to worry about Charlie's motivational speeches.

In the backyard, two muddy feet moved through the rain. The figure grabbed the shovel still on the ground where Clare left it, and began to dig.

On the way to his room, Charlie noticed Clare.

"I'm sorry again, Mom."

"I know it wasn't your idea, Charlie. You're better than that. I'm the one who should be apologizing."

"Trust me, I should apologize for a lot more. Do you mind if I take the Bible that was in the counter drawer?"

Clare gave him a look that said *I could care less.*

"No, not really. Why?"

"No reason, thanks."

Clare patted his shoulder and Charlie went back to his room. He couldn't help but think about how they hadn't told Clare about Mr. Jones. It started to feel like a huge lie not telling her what they did. Maybe that's what Meredith's note meant. The next Bible verse he read was Job 24:25, which he recognized easily. He pulled out his note from Meredith—the message matched the verse. He pulled his curtains aside, taking a good look at Meredith's house, which was dim and empty. He took his jacket from his blue desk chair, and made up his mind. He knew what he had to do.

Outside, a shadowy figure dug in their backyard, behind the closed blinds of the home. With the shovel, they finally dug enough around the patches of bushes and trees further back to uncover a body—which they were certain was Mr. Jones, Vivian's husband. His rotting head no longer rested in dirt but on the grass, visible for everyone to see. The being took something from their pocket—Vivian's necklace she wore to the party—and placed it next to his corpse. By the time another crack of thunder roared they were in the bushes, once again hidden.

Charlie made his way up the steps to Meredith's porch. He touched the cool wood against the front door.

"Goodbye, Meredith," he said, swallowing hard.

It didn't feel right to not say goodbye, and it felt more sincere being at her house, even though it was hard for him. It was crazy, and probably just in his head, but it even *smelled* like Meredith. It was like her spirit was still there, following Charlie. He would never forget her. It was insane to think how his first impression of Meredith differed from how he felt about her now. He wanted to stay longer, but knew in the matter of seconds Kate would probably figure out he was missing. He gave the front door one more touch, for the last time, then turned around for his house. As he turned, he noticed a light through the curtains of her house. He swore the house was pitch dark when he got there, unless the lamps were motion activated, but that didn't seem like the answer. As Charlie blinked, the light flickered off. Behind him the door squeaked halfway open, just by his touch, he assumed. There wasn't enough wind to open the door, but why wasn't it locked? It had just opened by Charlie touching the middle of it, not even the handle. Light flickered once more, this time from a lamp in the living room. He reached for the doorknob to close the door, the thunder scaring him. He heard something other than the creaking of the aged door.

He pressed his ear in between the crack in the door, listening hard. His heartbeat began to pound in his ears, but there was something else to be heard. He couldn't tell if there had been a television left on or what, but the faint sound of a human lingered in his ear, almost like a chanting of some kind. The door, almost on command, shut on Charlie's ear, the crunch of cartilage echoing through his mind. There had been a gush of wind a few seconds before, so it must have slammed the door shut. At the sound of the crunch he hurled the heavy door open, getting it away from his ear.

"Hello?"

The first thing he noticed on the ground, near the kitchen, was the basket of bread next to the wine stain on the floor. The house looked smaller without all the usual lights that had often heated the room with their brightness. He bent down at the bread, steam rushing from the basket. The bread was fresh, which made no sense to him. *What the heck is that,* he thought. As he bent down, there was a strange object under one of the kitchen chairs to his right. Something gravitated him towards it, and he wished he didn't look. Next to him was a doll with two heads. One of them had a Halo drawn on it, while the other had devil-looking horns coming from the top. Along the middle of the doll were dark segments drawn in black crayon that started at the bottom of the stomach and continued up the throat. They looked like train or tire tracks. The doll's temperature resembled an ice cube, and Charlie dropped it as soon as he attempted to pick it up.

What had all of this stuff been doing here? He thought about it for a moment, but nothing clicked. He knew what he was about to say was crazy, and he didn't expect a reply, but he still said it.

"Meredith?"

He let out a relieving breath, knowing she wouldn't just pop up and ask Charlie what was wrong. That would be impossible. The minute the word left his tongue; he did think he heard something, though. It was the same, faint chanting he heard at the door. It was only a smudge louder this time, but after about fifteen seconds, the word *me* could be heard. Charlie still figured a television was left on, but he couldn't fully convince himself of the idea. Things weren't making sense. He stood up, noticing a corner attachment to a hallway Kate and he hadn't seen while being with Meredith.

Lit only by a tiny, white candle, he decided to walk further, hoping there was just a TV on and he could turn it off before leaving. Something about the place made him more fascinated than before, and he couldn't get himself to leave. He had to figure out what was going on. He figured that was how Kate must have always felt—she always had to figure things out completely. On a small dresser halfway through the hallway stood several pictures colored in markers. The first that captured his attention was of a young girl, maybe eight years of age, in front of what looked like a couple of blinding lights. He tilted the picture at an angle and looked once more, the lights now looking more like the headlights of a car, but he couldn't fully tell.

The paper underneath showed a car—he realized the lights were headlights for sure—smashed into a tree. He almost didn't notice it, but near the tree was another young girl lying on her back, in the middle of the road. There was red crayon smeared on her. Something made him drop the paper. The same chanting picked up again, and he definitely heard *me*. He held his breath and closed his eyes, focusing on the noise, which lasted longer than usual. *Save me?* Charlie asked himself. It sure sounded like that. He heard the beginning once more, which was easy to realize the noise started with an *S*. The chanting began to sound desperate, like someone in need, but stopped. The candle in the hallway went dark, and the only light he could hope for was now the occasional lightning that sprung itself through the windows.

"Is anybody here?"

He couldn't believe he was still here, but he felt forced to stay. His feet physically would not move towards the door, but they had to.

"This is crazy," he said, leaving the pictures behind and using his strength to move towards the front door.

Once he reached the kitchen, the shatter sound of something heavy being dropped permeated through the walls. He had to turn back. The hallway seemed shorter as he moved his legs faster through it, and turned right. In his vision was a large, dark, brown desk. He took a step forward, noticing the pictures spilled over the desk. Some were he, and he could tell one was of Clare. One hung over the desk, almost falling into the trash bin next to it. They were burnt enough to make him struggle, but he could almost make out Vivian in one of the pictures in the trash. He dug through more, seeing one of Mr. Jones, as well as a picture of Michelle leaving Vivian's house out the back door. What alarmed Charlie more were the two pictures that sat next to the trash that were not as burnt through all the way, but just in the corners. They were of Kate and Clare. They showed Clare walking to Victor's house alone, while the other was of Kate talking with Jason outside. As he attempted touching those, his fingers tingled and the sensation of fifty small needles being jammed in his hand forced him to drop them.

"What is all of this," he whispered to himself.

The light Charlie stood in front of turned on and off by itself several times while he looked at the pictures, so he became somewhat accustomed to it. He took a look once more at Vivian and Mr. Jones' pictures, while behind him, only visible as the lamp flickered on, stood Sophie, staring at Charlie with red eyes. Her black dress absorbed much of the low-powered lamp, making her hardly visible. She was quiet; Charlie hadn't noticed her. By the time the light flickered off again, she was gone. Charlie couldn't help but feel like he wasn't alone. The sound of light footsteps flickered in Charlie's head, and he took his eyes off of the pictures. He wished there was more light, but wasn't going to attempt fixing the lamp. There was something eerie about it. The footsteps became louder, but maybe just in his head. He, one step at a time, made his way closer to the hallway he had come from. Sweat dripped from his forehead to his eyebrow. He hadn't realized how much hotter the house felt. As thunder roared outside, Meredith ran from the corner and charged at Charlie. In her hand was a knife, and her stomach was covered in blood, still dripping off of her body.

Charlie screamed louder than ever, and closed his eyes so tight it hurt. The footsteps disappeared, and opened one eye. Meredith was gone, but a sharp pain that started from Charlie's throat made its way to his foot. He looked down, blood dripping from his toe.

"She made me do it. She made me do it all!" he heard from behind him, in a chanting, high-pitched voice.

Finally, he saw the girl who he recognized as Mary staring at him, wearing the same white dress as she always did. She repeated the phrase, her face looking desperate. She pointed across the room, fear evident in her light blue eyes. He turned around, a girl identical to Mary with piercing red eyes looking at him. Her veins began to show, and her skin wrinkled. Her neck began to darken, and soon matched the color of her dress. He looked behind him—the girl in white was gone. Something about the girl in black was captivating. As he studied her, something looked strikingly familiar. Her bone structure, her mouth, even her hands—they all looked just like...Meredith.

"I told you to stay away from your family. Especially her," Sophie said.

The way she talked sounded like Meredith, too.

"What do you mean, *you* told me?" he asked.

Before she answered, she disappeared into the darkness as the lamp flickered off on command. Next to the trash bin was another picture, one Charlie hadn't seen. It was of Meredith in a black background, just staring. Her eyes were red. He bent down, touching it. There was a shadow next to him, and he dared to look up. Meredith stood over him—holding a red bouncy ball—making him fall back and hit his hand against the desk.

"Meredith? Please don't...I thought you died."

He looked into her eyes, which somehow looked bluer now...just like Mary's.

"Charlie, I've *been* dead."

He looked at the pictures near the trashcan and on the desk again. The sweat on his hands ran onto the carpet below him.

"Did you kill all of these people?"

He looked down and wiped his sweaty hands against his shirt, then looked back up. Meredith was no longer there.

"Please, Meredith!"

Someone behind him answered.

"She made me do it! She controlled me, Charlie!"

It was Mary, crying out again in desperation and fear. Charlie's head spun, and he couldn't make sense of this no matter how he thought of it. He waited for her to d again, but she stayed.

"Who? Who made you?"

"Save me, please!" she said.

"Who made you do all of this?"

She pointed at her heart and breathed heavier.

"She did—Sop..."

Before she could finish, she collapsed, her light body making a loud noise as it hit the ground.

Charlie's body went cold and his spine tingled at the screeching, chilling, and raw hitch-pitched scream that followed. He covered his ears, and attempted to escape. He ran towards the hallway, when something grabbed his leg. His toe still throbbed and bled, and his body fell onto a black rug that felt like it swallowed him up. It was probably since his head was spinning, but he could have sworn there was a face on the rug, staring at him. His grip on the rug tightened, and he tried to pull up his heavy, exhausted body. But in a blink the carpet snapped and, as if under someone's control, was thrown and pulled, thrusting him backward.

"What...why are you doing all of this?" he said, his voice tightening.

"Because he killed me," she said.

"Who?"

"Your dad."

The girl disappeared, but he could still hear her. He could even feel her breath, which was hot and stuck to him.

"What? That's impossible—my dad died!"

The girl in white appeared. She was in tears.

"After he killed me! Charlie, she did it on purpose, she didn't save me from that car! She took control of me; I didn't want to do any of it. It's her fault—she wanted revenge!"

"Revenge? My dad is dead! Why kill everyone else?"

The room went quiet, and Charlie's words pounded in his head. Was everything over? He thought so, until Mary talked once more, sounding out of breath.

"You were different, Charlie. You read my note, and understood it. You're stronger than her."

"Than who?"

"Her, Charlie. Sophie! She can't get to you! You're stronger than me. That's why I warned you about Kate—she's her target. Sophie killed my mother, Charlie! She would have killed my brother if he wasn't in jail or running away so much."

"Why didn't you tell me all of this?"

"I couldn't..."

"Why not?"

She looked at her stomach, and shut her eyes.

"She's everywhere."

"What are talking about—"?

"—I tried. At the party, when you were going to the bathroom."

Charlie played that night in his head. He remembered going to the bathroom, seeing Meredith near the door, knowing somehow he was going to enter. What had she said to him? With all that had happened, his memory pretty much exploded. Was it about doing something often at night? *No, evening.* He knew the first word started with an *S,* but he couldn't understand how that was Mary telling him about Sophie. He mentally told himself to wait, noticing her name started with an *S* also. *In evening,* he told himself, thinking harder. He remembered there was something about going to the bathroom mentioned...*peeing.* Before he mapped out the scene more, he thought about the first letters of those words...*S, P,* and *E*—all letters in Sophie's name. He didn't have time to think more, but had the realization that Mary told him that night Sophie was there, controlling her.

"No! Please, no," she said.

Charlie didn't understand. Just then the lamp flickered faster than ever. A strange sound came from the bulb, and the light made his eyes spin. The bulb exploded, sending him into total darkness. Mary was silent. He felt something push him to the hard ground. All he heard was wind rocking from outside the taped windows, the plastic cover moving like a ghost. Lightning illuminated the room, allowing enough light for Charlie to watch, in horror, of Sophie's face inches from his. The image of her red, evil eyes burned deep into his mind. Once the room darkened, her face was gone. When he turned his head, there was a dark figure standing at the end of the hallway, still as a statue. He started with his knees, and dug them into the deep, black rug. He used the dresser near him to help him stand, still staring at the dark figure. An icy chill ran up his spine as he heard Sophie's voice.

"Come on, Charlie. Forget her, and let's stop fighting. Join me," she said.

Her screechy words sounded tempting, even though he didn't want them to. What did she want him to join her in?

"You can't handle all of this alone. Let me help you," she said.

He noticed Sophie's hand reach out, but she stayed at the end of the hallway.

"Leave me alone," Charlie demanded.

"You won't have to worry about anything—not Clare, Kate, or remembering all the horrible things you did."

"Shut up."

Charlie heard Sophie breathing harder, becoming angrier. The second of silence was broken as Sophie charged from the end of the hall towards him at full speed, letting out an ear-shattering scream. She tightened a grip on his short neck.

"You killed my father!'

Charlie felt a vein in his throat pop. Unbearable pressure built up in his head, and he kicked his feet.

"I'm sorry," he tried to breath out.

"You can either accept me, and everything will be over, or be tortured for the rest of your unimportant life. You're nothing without me," she said, spitting on him.

Her words sounded so harsh and...*evil.* Something about her made him think—for a mere second—she was right. He needed to join Sophie and let go of all the crazy murder theories. It didn't matter what happened to Mary, who had desperately wanted freedom from Sophie's control. All of that swarmed his mind in a mere second, but he tried helplessly to resist those thoughts. With his hands and all energy, he grabbed her remaining hand and dug the sharp nails into her skin, making her growl and scream. However, her grip loosened for enough time to reach for the trash bin near Charlie, under the brown desk covered in pictures. His hands brushed the side of it, and Sophie's grip tightened more than before. His heels dug into the floor as he tried to boost himself one more inch, in order to get a good grip on the bin. Charlie felt numb, but refused to die or give into Sophie—which was probably worse. He never encountered true evil—he didn't even realize it existed—until now. Using his pinky, he gripped the top of the trashcan and hoped for the best. Every muscle in his body contracted more than ever, and he thrusted the metal bin at Sophie, hitting her jaw. Her grip loosened and she fell on her side for three seconds. As Charlie forced himself to stand up, his eyes went to a picture taped to the bottom of the trashcan. It looked like a child colored it, just like those from the dresser. He recognized the figure as his father. The man sat in a ditch with red crayon smeared over his arms, where something that looked like a cut, or broken, bottle of some kind stuck out. In the left corner of the picture was a car with blinding headlights that matched the others. He regretted taking those seconds to look at the picture, and knew he had to turn away and run. Even though he heard Sophie slither towards him, he finally felt the doorknob at the front door. *Thank God.* His fingers turned the knob, but it didn't open. It made a strange noise and refused to budge. There had to be another way out. He didn't have time to worry about how much his throat hurt or what else popped in him, but his eyes stayed on the Bible resting on the kitchen counter that he had seen when he visited Meredith—uh, Mary. Another lamp flickered on and off, and his eyes burned when he saw Sophie coming towards him closer and closer every time the light turned back on. There was nothing else to do. He was going to die. Nothing could save him at this point; he really thought differently before. He must have been wrong. Those thoughts poured into his mind, and he didn't fight them any longer.

The lamp flickered once more, Sophie visible and crawling closer to him. She was now feet away. Finally something inside of Charlie sparked.

"Just leave me—and Mary—alone! We don't need you! Go away," he said before running again, even though he knew it was helpless.

Every light on the house turned on in unison, and flickered together.

"Charlie, I need to tell you something," Kate said at home as she walked into his room.

She needed to tell him about her plan to call the police, and run her script by him.

"Charlie?"

The room was empty. Lights shone through his window, but quickly turned off. She took steps closer and opened the curtains fully. What was Charlie doing at Meredith's house this late? What could he possibly be doing—she was dead! Something was wrong. She looked closer, seeing Charlie run through the house, looking back ten times as if there was a ghost behind him. Of course, she knew ghosts weren't real, but that's what it was like. Nevertheless, she had to do something. Without putting her shoes on, she slammed the door loud enough, Clare probably heard from across the house.

The lights cut off, and Charlie heard mumbling and whispering. It was Sophie, but he couldn't understand any of it. He covered his ears and looked for...*something* to help him. The voices followed behind.

"Just let me show you what I can do for you," he heard in part of the whispering. He hit a dead in the house, then ran for the kitchen once more. The floor had trails of blood from Charlie, but he didn't notice. His eyes fixed on the Bible once more, and he felt something pulling him closer to It. His pulse slowed when he put his hands on the pages, and he let out a huge breath. The voices halted.

"Help me," he whispered.

Charlie took the Bible and ran. Maybe the door would somehow work now. The lamp turned back on and he saw a shadow on the wall. It was tall and had claw-like hands.

"Charlie!" Kate yelled as she approached the house, although unaware of anything besides some weird flickering lights inside. She was just feet away from the front steps.

The only sound Charlie heard was Sophie's scream once more. He reached for the door handle, but noticed the shadow coming closer to him at full speed. Too scared, he got into the position of a ball and held the Bible tighter than he kept his eyes shut. He hoped and waited for something good to happen. He didn't feel anything, and opened his eyes.

Kate stepped up the third step. She heard some kind of awful scream, but it couldn't have been Charlie. It was too high-pitched. The next second, something hit her, and she flew back off the stairs. Her back smashed into the concrete. Her bones felt broken. There hadn't been anything there but wind—how could that have knocked her off her feet? Kate felt her eyes shut.

Charlie looked down at the Bible and smiled. The lamp that once flickered remained on, without turning off again. He took several seconds to get back on his feet, but Charlie got up.

"Thank you," he heard a voice say. He turned to see Mary staring at him, looking overjoyed. She was clothed in a red dress.

"You beat it," she said.

She walked to him, and touched his wrist.

"I knew you were different. Are you okay?"

Her gaze was on his scratches and the blood dripping from him.

"I'm perfect."

They smiled at each other. She reached out her hand, and Charlie cupped his in hers. Charlie wasn't a normal kid. He went through a lot. He was almost framed and charged for murder, and even thought his sister was capable of such. But that stuff didn't matter—none of it did. He was a new person.

Thunder echoed in Kate's ears. She found her body bent in ways a human couldn't normally stay. She raised both arms in unison. Her body stood up, and there was something different about her. There wasn't any pain in her body anymore. She took a deep breath, whispered and mumbled something under her breath, and stared at Meredith's house through her piercing, red eyes.

There are two sides to every person. You choose to be controlled by either one of them. Getting to the good means beating the evil within us. Some find it impossible, and some lucky ones figure it out.

www.ingramcontent.com/pod-product-compliance
Lightning Source LLC
LaVergne TN
LVHW041220080526
838199LV00082B/1331